THE ITALIAN'S
TROPHY MISTRESS

by

Diana Hamilton

Diana Hamilton is a true romantic and fell in love with her husband at first sight. They still live in the fairytale Tudor house where they raised their three children. Now the idyll is shared with eight rescued cats and a puppy. But, despite an often chaotic lifestyle, ever since she learned to read and write Diana has had her nose in a book – either reading or writing one – and plans to go on doing just that for a very long time to come.

CHAPTER ONE

'DARLINGS—have you heard? Henry Croft is divorcing his third wife and moving on to number four!'

Across the candlelit dinner table Claudia Neill's black eyes sparked with what Bianca Jay could only describe as malicious glee, and a shiver inched coldly down her spine as Cesare's younger sister continued, the sympathetic curve of her mouth at odds with the spiteful relish of her tone. 'Amanda's absolutely gutted, of course. The poor thing's been living on a knife-edge since Henry was photographed at the Oscars with that busty little film star—whose name escapes me for the moment—but you know the one. Bit parts, mostly, huge blonde hair down to her waist. Used to sing in a pop group. Mind you, poor Amanda will get lots of lovely alimony—'

Claudia gave a languid shrug, her naked shoulders smooth as silk above the little black slip dress she was wearing. 'However big the settlement, it won't make up for being dumped for a younger, flashier model, will it? But what did poor Amanda expect? Marry a man with a roving eye, an image to live up to and more money than he knows what to do with and you can think yourself lucky if you last more than a couple of years!'

5

Was she supposed to answer that? Bianca wondered grittily as she tried to ignore the sudden lurch of her stomach. For the hundredth time she wished she hadn't so weakly agreed to come. But Cesare had told her, 'I'm sorry about this, especially as it's my first night back in London. But it's my little sister's birthday and I promised to give her dinner at my apartment. There'll only be the four of us. You, me, Claudia and Alan. And they won't stay late; I believe their baby-sitter won't stay beyond eleven—she can't take the strain of trying to get those two little monsters to stay in bed! And then there will be just the two of us.'

And, as always, she had found him dangerously impossible to resist.

Throughout the evening she'd been thinking of that danger. It was a subject that had been occupying her mind almost constantly over the past few weeks. To tell him their six-month relationship was over before she got in too deep, did herself some serious damage. Or go on as they were, knowing that the day would inevitably come when he would tell *her* their affair was over. It was a decision she simply had to make.

'Of course—' Claudia was practically purring now, smiling sideways at her doting husband, one hand dipping a silver spoon into her strawberry sorbet, the other playing with the sapphire pendant that had been Cesare's birthday gift to her '—Alan's not wealthy enough to trade me in, so I guess I'm pretty safe.' A fluting laugh, as artificial as tinsel, then her dark eyes fed on Bianca's suddenly pale face. 'And at least you

and Cesare know where you stand, don't you, my darlings? All the fun of a temporary affair with none of
the chores of marriage.'

'Chores?' Alan lifted one sandy brow in an imita-
tion of pained outrage, and Claudia rolled her dark
eyes.

'Oh, you know, *caro*—squabbling over my dress
allowance, dealing with the twins' tantrums, organising babysitters—'

But Bianca wasn't listening. That had been a direct
dig at her mistress status. It wasn't a status she was
remotely proud of. A rich man's trophy, to be paraded
around all the right places, casually introduced to his
circle of exalted friends, and just as casually dropped
when someone new and exciting piqued his interest.

She had met Cesare Andriotti through her PR work,
organising the opening shindig for the latest in the
string of luxury hotel, leisure and conference com-
plexes owned by his illustrious family and bearing the
Andriotti name.

It had been lust at first sight, she recalled, ignoring
the friendly bickering going on between Claudia and
her husband.

She'd known it was dangerous, not what she
wanted. She was career-driven, independent, and had
no time for a steady personal relationship—a husband
and family wouldn't fit in with the largely unsociable
hours she worked, with the often draining emotional
commitments she already had.

And how many times had she told herself that

Cesare Andriotti was the kind of man she had most reason to despise?

Countless.

Wealthy beyond the dreams of avarice, drop-dead handsome, with barrow-loads of Italian charisma and the almost indefinable touch of arrogance that sent delicious shivers down the spine of any female in his vicinity. The kind of men who had everything, who took mistresses, showered them with gifts, and felt they had the perfect right to drop them flat—very politely, with oodles of charm, of course—just when they felt like it.

She had tried to keep him at arm's length—at least, that was what she had told herself she'd been doing—but within a month of first meeting him she'd become his mistress. She simply hadn't been able to help herself. He had overwhelmed her, ridden roughshod over each and every one of her objections—moral, practical and self-preserving.

His eyes were on her; she could feel them. Her spine tingled. He'd been watching her ever since his sister had made that barbed comment about them having only a temporary affair.

She refused to turn her head and look at him, meet those incredibly sexy, slate-grey moody eyes, let her own eyes linger on that passionate mouth or devour the lean and whippy lines of that elegantly clad, seemingly indolent body. To do so would mean she would be lost, the ever-hardening resolve to end their affair blown apart in her body's consuming need for him.

'Might I ask a favour, sir?' Alan asked gruffly, reddening as he amended, 'Cesare.'

Alan Neill was Head of Accounts for the UK side of the huge financial empire, had fallen in love with Claudia Andriotti when she'd been visiting Cesare at his London apartment and had never quite come to terms with the fact that his boss was his brother-in-law.

Bianca's heart went out to him.

At thirty-four years of age, heading up the Andriotti business empire since his father's retirement four years ago, Cesare struck awe into the hearts and minds of everyone who met him. Alan was out of his depth. He was thoroughly nice, too stolid and loyal ever to even think of betraying his pretty, temperamental wife; Claudia would never have to worry about being traded in.

At his wife's pointed arch of one fine, dark brow Alan stumbled on, 'Would it be possible for us to have the company jet in early August? It seems a bit much to ask but, the fact is, the twins would be a nightmare on a commercial flight. Won't keep still, into everything, and you know how shrill three-year-old boys are when they get over-excited.' He pushed his fingers through his thick sandy hair and made an abortive attempt at a lightly relaxed laugh. 'I'd hate to inflict them on fare-paying passengers.'

'Darling—' Claudia placed a delicate, scarlet-tipped hand on her husband's sleeve '—do stop rambling. Of course Cesare won't mind.' She smiled at her brother, her long lashes fluttering. 'Mamma and Papa insist we take the boys out to Calabria for their wedding anniversary in August. And I'm quite sure you have your orders, too! So, if we may, we'll join you on the flight out and back again? But if you can't make it—' she pouted prettily '—then please may we have the use of the Lear?'

Bianca covered her wineglass with her long, tapering fingers as Cesare made a move to refill it, looking directly ahead, anywhere but at him, carefully keeping a slight smile on her face, her expression on the politely interested side of bland.

But she wasn't listening to a word of the affectionate family conversation. Claudia had probably been twisting her big brother round her tiny finger since she had first learned to walk!

Any arrangements that were being made for the family reunion wouldn't, of course, include her.

Meeting up with his sister and brother-in-law on one or two social occasions had been unavoidable, hence her inclusion in this private birthday celebration. She was important to him for the nights they could spend together. For now. But not important enough to be included in a visit to his parents.

She hadn't met Cesare's twin nephews, whose precocious misdemeanours were now being so fondly discussed. But she'd heard about them.

Right at the start of their affair Cesare had told her, in response to her probably gauche comment that she wasn't into long-term commitment, 'Neither am I.

Why should I marry? My sister has already done her duty and presented the family with twin boys.'

His long fingers had been relaxed on the stem of his wineglass, the slight smile that had always both unnerved her and captivated her playing around his mouth as his eyes had slid lingeringly over her features. 'Our arrangement suits me perfectly.'

At least he was honest, she thought tiredly as she watched the waiter from the firm of caterers Cesare always used when he entertained at his London apartment glide towards them with a tray of coffee. As she knew to her cost, many men in his rarefied financial position married and divorced with monotonous regularity.

That conversation had taken place back in the early days, she reminded herself as the waiter deferentially placed a gold-rimmed coffee cup in front of her. But things were changing. Cesare was beginning to want things she didn't dare to give.

And now was the time to make a clean and decisive break before she was left with a shattered heart, aching regrets and a desperate yearning for things that could never be, things she hadn't wanted in the first place, shouldn't even be thinking about wanting now.

Placing her linen napkin on the table amongst the beautiful china, the Venetian glass, she murmured, 'This has been delightful, but I really must go. Enjoy the rest of your birthday, Claudia.'

A polite social smile on her face, Bianca rose to her feet. She was shaking inside with the enormity of what she now knew she had to do, but no one must know it.

Claudia's eyes were bright, almost chillingly knowing as she uttered with obviously false regret, 'Darling, must you? Really? I would hate to think Alan and I had cramped your style!'

'Not at all,' Bianca made herself reply lightly and turned to Alan, who had risen awkwardly to his feet. 'Please. Enjoy the rest of the evening,' she said, before forcing herself to walk out of the elegantly appointed dining room with at least the outward appearance of unhurried grace.

Cesare was following, as she had known he would. She heard the scrape of his chair as he rose from the table, the low murmur of his velvety voice as he made his excuses, and her stomach twisted sharply inside her.

In the adjoining vast sitting room Bianca snatched her mobile from her slim evening bag and punched in the numbers of her usual minicab firm with shaking fingers. Her breath was coming in rapid, shallow gasps as she ended the call and Cesare, right beside her now, said, '*Cara mia*, what is wrong? You were to stay with me tonight. Don't go. For three weeks I have ached for you.'

He placed both hands on her shoulders and she felt her body go rigid. His low-pitched sexy drawl swamped her with longing, the possessive pressure of his fingers burned through the tawny-coloured silk that clothed her shoulders, reinforcing the mindlessly driven need to turn in his arms, loop her hands against the back of his beautifully shaped proud head, tangle her fingers in the thick, silky luxuriance of his jet-black hair and drown in the passion of his kiss.

Fighting against the incredible danger, Bianca moved away, putting much-needed space between them, blinking fiercely to stop the prickle of tears becoming a flood. He'd asked her what was wrong. Everything was wrong. Their no-strings, light-hearted affair was becoming much deeper and darker, at least as far as she was concerned.

She was growing too dependent on him, inclined to be unreasonably angered and hurt when he had to cancel a date, missing him until she ached all over, could think of nothing but him when he was out of the country, her ears on permanent alert for the phone call that would tell her he was back in London.

She was falling fathoms deep in love with him, that was the answer to his question!

But no way could she tell him. No way!

Love wasn't part of their 'arrangement'.

A long, easy stride brought him in front of her. The slightly musky, slightly sharp scent of him engulfed her, pushing the words she knew she had to say to him back down her throat, making the struggle to reassemble them well nigh impossible.

'Stay,' he said gently. 'I need you. If there's a problem—with work, with anything—I'll handle it.' The slight but inescapable pressure of his fingertip beneath her chin forced her eyes to meet his. Slate-grey enigmas fringed with thick dark lashes above the proud jut of his cheekbones, the thinly arrogant blade of his nose at certain odds with the savage passion of his beautiful mouth. He was so shatteringly handsome he made her heart ache.

His automatic assumption that he could effortlessly solve problems that would tie lesser mortals in knots made her throat tighten with near-hysterical reaction. It had nothing to do with wealth or position and everything to do with his sheer masculine virility, the dynamism of his personality.

'I can't.' Bianca managed the reply to his request through lips so numb they felt as if they didn't belong to her, her eyes still held to the mesmerising force field of his.

'Why? I thought it was all arranged.' His long, lean fingers curved gently around her jaw and his head lowered just a little. A preliminary to kissing her senseless?

Unwilling to take that risk, she jerked her head away, dragging in an anguished breath. Of course she'd meant to stay, drawn to his presence like the proverbial moth to the flame, saved only by antennae that had sensed and finally and unmistakably understood the danger before it had been too late.

Her fingers digging into the soft kid of her slim evening bag, she mentally formed the words that once spoken would be completely final.

He would accept what she said with a word or two of polite regret; he had too much pride to ask her to reconsider. From the moment the words were out it would be over. There would be no going back.

A steadying breath, a straightening of her shoulders, a flick of a tongue-tip over lips that felt stiff and dry. 'It's over, Cesare. I won't be seeing you again.'

There, it was out, the bald statement that would leave her with some self-respect, that would save her heart from permanent damage. It had taken all her resolve to say the words that had felt as if they were being dragged from her, dropping like stones into an atmosphere that had suddenly become charged with more than the effect of her tightly wired nerves.

The tension was coming from him now, a subtle hardening of his strong jawline, a momentary flicker in the depths of those enigmatic eyes, a lifting of the dark head, emphasising the whippy power of a six-foot frame that was outrageously masculine. It made her shudder in instinctive response.

Cesare gritted his teeth against a violent internal surge that seemed to be tearing him apart and had to use all his self-control to prevent himself from taking her in his arms and kissing her lovely mouth until she retracted her words.

She couldn't leave him. He wouldn't let her!

Pulling a sharp breath through his nostrils, he closed his eyes briefly before allowing them to dwell on her face. Beautiful. There was a touch of the exotic about her creamy skin, the smooth black hair, lush mouth and long amber eyes, her slender, perfectly formed body clothed tonight in glowing tawny silk.

She couldn't disguise the way her soft lips trembled, but there was a cold light of determination in her eyes that told him that, although the touch of his lips to hers, the slide of his hands, moving slowly from her slender shoulders to the globes of her breasts so tantalisingly delineated beneath the thin silky fabric, would ignite the conflagration of passion they were both helpless before, nothing would change her decision.

A vague uneasiness at the way their relationship had been going had been eating away at him for many weeks. Her refusal to move in with him, the look of pain when she'd refused the gifts that had been meant to give her pleasure, the way she had never once invited him into her home, her soft evasiveness when he'd questioned her about her family, her upbringing, her hopes for the future.

He knew as little about her now as he had done when he'd first met her and had known, with shattering immediacy, that he'd wanted her in his bed.

Despite the gossip, he hadn't had as many mistresses as he'd been credited with. And when the time for parting had come, as it inevitably had, there had been no rancour on either side, no heartache.

So was it the mystery of her that made her different? He didn't know. He only knew that he had never felt like this before. Emptied of his normal assurance, his self-sufficiency, filled instead with a yearning pain.

Denying the temptation to reach out and touch her, evoke the magic that would keep her with him just one more time, he thrust his hands into the pockets of his narrow-fitting black trousers and said with an impulsiveness that rocked him back on his heels, 'Marry me, Bianca.'

CHAPTER TWO

Marry him!

The shock of Cesare's proposal had turned Bianca
to stone, the only movement detectable being the frantic beating of her heart as it hammered against her ribs.
Only the arrival of Denton, Cesare's manservant, a
few seconds later, snatched her out of the fantasy land
where she and Cesare were bound together by love
until death did them part and plunged her back into
stark reality.

'Your cab's arrived, Miss Jay.'

Just five cockney-accented words were all it took to
clear her head, strengthen her resolve, move her out
of the paralysing shock that had held her immobile,
allow her to focus on Denton's impassive, homely features, force out a pallid smile, a word of thanks, turn
again to Cesare, not meeting his eyes, and push the
single word 'goodbye' through her lips.

And walk from the room, anguish a tight band
around her heart, leaving behind the man she was
growing to love with more passion than reason, point-
edly ignoring his offer of marriage as if it were beneath her consideration, that insult the final and firmest
nail in the coffin of their relationship.

As the cab made uneven progress towards Hampstead

through the late-evening traffic Bianca pressed her fingertips against the burning pressure of her eyelids. She would not cry. She couldn't allow herself that luxury. And even thinking about that shock proposal of marriage was counter-productive. If anything, it made everything worse. Far worse.

A permanent relationship was the last thing Cesare wanted; hadn't he told her that much?

So why that shock proposal of marriage?

Shuddering as her stomach tied itself in nauseating knots, she forced herself to face facts, to find an answer to that question. He obviously hadn't yet tired of their nights of blazing, unforgettable passion, she ticked off mentally. Cesare still wanted her physically, perhaps because the time they'd spent together had been governed by the foreign travel made necessary by his business commitments, her refusal to move in with him, her insistence that when she stayed with him she left at dawn, alone, taking a cab back to the home she shared with her mother.

So their time together had been snatched—and inevitably all the more precious for that. There had been nothing routine or predictable about their affair. Therefore, it followed, Cesare hadn't yet grown bored.

Hence the surprise proposal. Bind her legally until he tired of her. It was the sort of thing that was taken for granted in the ultra-sophisticated circles he moved in. The sort of thing that brought devastation in its wake, as she knew only too well.

It was over, she lectured herself staunchly as the

cab drew into the street where she lived. She had done the right, the sensible thing and now she had to forget Cesare Andriotti, forget the brief dead-end affair that had started to mean far too much to her, and concentrate on the immediate and problematic future.

Giving mental thanks for Aunt Jeanne's willingness to be co-opted, Bianca paid off the driver and stood for a moment in the warm late-May evening, readying herself to enter the house.

She had to put her own anguish aside and get to grips with the love and duty she owed to her mother. Without Aunt Jeanne's presence, she reminded herself, she would have been unable to attend Claudia's birthday dinner party this evening, an event which had helped her to finally make up her mind about ending her affair with Cesare.

And without her aunt's promise to keep an eye on her sister, Bianca's mother, she would have had to have asked her boss, Stazia, for an extended period of leave, at least until her mother's problems had been resolved.

Expelling a short sigh, she turned to face the house that wouldn't be theirs for much longer.

The steps up to the white-painted door sheltered by a stone pediment, the empty window-boxes on either side that she really should have planted up weeks ago, the elegantly curtained windows. The desirable façade proclaimed respectability but hid anything but.

As if to reinforce her wry observation the door in front of her was flung open and a golden-skinned

youth wearing a singlet and boxer shorts half fell, half
hurtled down the steps followed by sundry articles of
clothing accompanied by her mother's cut-glass tones,
now raised in ringing, withering scorn, 'Damned
sprog! What do you think I am? Desperate?' Her tone
lowered scathingly. 'And a word of advice—polish up
your wares before you attempt to sell them.'

Backlit by the hall illumination Helene Jay's tall,
bone-thin figure, wrapped in a filmy, ruffled robe, was
bristling with outrage, her carefully tinted copper hair
writhing about the ageing beauty of her far too heavily
made-up face.

Ignoring the youth who was scrabbling around for
his scattered belongings, Bianca mounted the steps.
Her heart was somewhere near the soles of her feet
and she wanted to collapse into floods of tears. To
weep for what she had thrown away tonight and what
she faced in the immediate future.

But letting go was out of the question. For the larger
part of her twenty-five years she had had to be the
stronger part of the mother-daughter relationship and
now her mother needed every bit of support she could
give her.

Two weeks ago her mother had been having the
contents of her stomach unceremoniously pumped out.
An overdose of sleeping pills and vast quantities of
alcohol. 'One teeny drink too many and I forgot I'd
already taken my pills—too silly of me, darling,' had
been the excuse she'd feebly proffered.

But Bianca wasn't so sure. Approaching her fiftieth

birthday, no regular man in her life, her once fantastic looks fading rapidly, Helene Jay was pitifully vulnerable. Her always volatile temperament was daily growing more brittle. Anything could happen.

Reaching her mother's side, Bianca took her arm, inwardly flinching at the extreme thinness of the flesh beneath her fingers, and turned her gently back into the hall, closing the door behind them.

'Helene—don't—' she exhorted, her voice riven with compassion as a sudden storm of sobs shook the older woman's frame. She couldn't bear to see her mother like this, her thick black mascara smudged into panda-like circles, her scarlet lipstick gravitating into the fine lines around her mouth.

'That little creep was a gigolo! I had no idea! How could I have?' she wailed brokenly. 'He assumed I had to pay for male company!'

'Then he's obviously either completely stupid, or blind.' Bianca did her utmost to soothe the already battered ego, her shaking fingers reaching a tissue from her bag to mop the mascara-streaked tears from her mother's face, murmuring with what she hoped was the right balance of humour and concern, 'I thought you and Jeanne were settled for the night, watching television.'

Helene jerked her head away, her recent humiliation momentarily forgotten. 'That programme you said was unmissable was deadly boring and Jeanne's got no conversation to speak of—discussing knitting patterns and recipes is her idea of sparkling repartee—and do stop treating me like a child, darling. I know you mean well, but it can be stultifying! I needed a drink and as this house has become a positive temperance hall I went out to get one.'

And unknowingly picked up a gigolo, Bianca thought despairingly. Years ago her mother had never lacked attentive male company but as time had crept inexorably onwards adoring lovers had become demeaning one-night stands, her spending on the latest fashions more incautious, her drinking habits more injurious.

This latest incident with the golden youth who had wanted payment for services about to be rendered could be the final nudge that could tip the fading, once fabulously beautiful woman clear over the edge.

And where the heck was Jeanne?

As if in answer to Bianca's unspoken question a stout, elderly woman descended the stairs, tying the belt of a serviceable fawn dressing gown around what passed for her waist.

'I heard shouting—such a commotion! I came as soon as I could.'

As soon as she'd located her false teeth and removed her curlers, Bianca translated wearily. To Aunt Jeanne respectability was all.

'I heard a man's voice, calling you names—and you screeching.' Her mild blue eyes hardened as she took in the ravaged state of her younger sister's face. 'You told me, Helene, that you were tired and fancied an early night. So I went up early, too.' She vented a long sigh. 'You tricked me. I didn't come all this way to look after you to be made a fool of.'

Cesare bade his sister and brother-in-law goodnight, impatient to end the evening that had dragged so slowly since Bianca's departure carefully concealed behind a bland smile that didn't reach his eyes.

The caterers had left half an hour ago and Denton was doing some unnecessary clearing up in the kitchen. Curtly dismissing him for the night, Cesare turned off the lights and headed for his study.

Normally, the quiet, book-lined room was a peaceful oasis in his hectic working life. No fax machines, computer screens or telephones to spoil the relaxing atmosphere. Whatever the pressures, he made it a rule never to bring his work back to whichever home he happened to be using at the moment.

But tonight, he knew, he wouldn't be able to relax anywhere on earth until he could get his head round what had happened.

Dumping an inch of malt whisky in a squat crystal tumbler, he paced the room, his stride rapid and edgy, anger holding his shoulders rigid.

She had said it was over. Just like that.

In his experience it didn't happen that way. His occasional affairs had been ended by him, the demise carefully signalled weeks in advance. The parting was amicable with gentle words of regret, a lavish gift—a car, jewellery, an exotic holiday—according to the lady in question's preferences.

But never like this. Never!

And never before he was ready to end it!

Slamming his empty glass down on the leather-topped desk, he scowled at the spines of the books on the shelves, not seeing them. The anger that raged through him in a roaring torrent demanded release.

And where in the name of all that was sacred had that proposal of marriage come from? *Porca miseria*— his mind must have gone walkabout! The words had slipped out without any direction from his brain, shocking him.

His hands balled into fists and his jaw clenched until his teeth ached. She had simply ignored what he'd said. Not by a flicker of those fabulous lashes had she revealed that his monumentally crazy offer of marriage had made the slightest impact,

Many women would have killed their own grand-mothers to hear those words from his lips!

Bianca Jay had simply looked through him and walked away!

No one, but no one, humiliated Cesare Andriotti and got away with it!

His ebony brows flared as he bit out an expletive in rawly vented Italian. Then, collecting himself, he dragged in a deep breath, meant to be calming but not quite hitting the mark.

He had wanted Bianca Jay from the very first mo-ment of seeing her. She hadn't been a pushover but he'd got what he'd wanted from her in the end. But somehow, on a level he'd never encountered before, it had been far more complicated than the slaking of physical lust within the confines of a sophisticated affair.

The beautiful, elusive Bianca had begun to intrigue him. In bed they shared a mind-blowing ecstasy but out of it she kept him at a distance, never letting him get to really know her.

She'd flatly refused to move in with him and put their relationship on a semi-permanent basis, and had made it abundantly plain that she would accept none of the gifts he had instinctively wanted to shower on her, had refused to speak of her background, her family, easily and prettily changing the subject whenever he'd brought it up.

And although he'd increasingly wanted to know what made her the woman she was he'd respected her need for privacy, battening down his ever-growing desire to solve the mystery of her, pin down the elusiveness that was part of her tantalising contribution to their relationship.

Impatiently sloshing another inch of whisky into his glass, he took it to his desk and extracted a slim notebook from one of the drawers. Riffling through it, he found the number he wanted.

What had happened this evening had changed all the rules. Respecting her privacy was now completely out of the frame.

Sitting on the comfortably upholstered swivel chair, he reached for the phone, his shoulders relaxing, his eyes darkening and narrowing as his anger hardened into something darker, needier.

Don't get mad, get even!

'It's not going to work, is it?' Jeanne said decisively as she stirred the third spoonful of sugar into her breakfast coffee.

Dressed this morning in a light tweed skirt and cotton blouse, every iron-grey curl in its designated place, she looked what she was: sensible, stolid and utterly reliable. Sighing, Bianca had to agree with her aunt's blunt statement. In the past she had coped alone with her mother's growing excesses, her startling mood changes, but after the overdose episode she had been really frightened.

For the first time ever she'd sought outside help in the shape of her widowed Aunt Jeanne. Her amber eyes misted with tears as she recalled her aunt's immediate offer. 'She can stay with me in Bristol while you wind things up that end and find somewhere else to live. And I'll spend the next week or two with you until she's feeling more herself, keep an eye on her while you're out at work. From the sound of it she shouldn't be left too much on her own.'

Bianca had grasped the offer with both grateful hands. The lease on this house expired in a couple of months. Hunting for a flat she could afford, holding down her demanding job, deciding what to do about the furnishings—all while coping with her mother's problems—would have been a nightmare.

Newly discharged from hospital, feeling frail and needy, Helene had listlessly agreed. But on the evidence of last night's return to her former addictions, alcohol and men, it was obvious that she wouldn't settle for five minutes in her sister's tidy little semi in a quiet road on the outskirts of Bristol.

'I love my sister but I can't take the responsibility; it wouldn't be fair on either of us,' Jeanne admitted. 'What she needs is professional help—one of those fancy clinics you read about, where film stars and footballers go to get themselves sorted out.'

'If only!' Bianca gave a wry smile as she passed her aunt a rack of fresh toast and sat to pour herself some desperately needed strong hot coffee. 'She refuses to see her GP about her problems, mainly because she won't admit she has any. But she'd probably go for a fancy, up-market clinic. It would suit her image!' She took a grateful sip of the aromatic brew in her cup and added prosaically, 'Unfortunately, there's no way we could afford that sort of treatment.'

'Nothing left of the settlement?'

'That went years ago.' Bianca lifted her shoulders in a weary shrug. Her mother's divorce settlement had been recklessly spent on the latest designer clothes, lavish parties, an endless supply of drink.

'Then ask your father to pay for treatment. He's extremely wealthy, by all accounts. And it's mostly his fault she's the way she is.' Jeanne spread butter lavishly on her toast. 'You know, I always used to envy my little sister. When she married Conrad Jay I thought she had everything. Wealth beyond her wildest dreams—a bit ''new money'', but you can't have everything. At least his financial clout bought their way into the most glittering social circles. She was so beautiful and I was plain. But now I'm glad—about being plain.' She took a healthy bite. 'If you've never had any looks you can't lose them and get all bitter and twisted about it. That said, you should approach your father for help.'

'No.' The refusal was instinctive. Seeing Jeanne's quick frown, Bianca knew she had to elaborate and excuse her apparent stubbornness.

Although the sisters had kept in touch through the years, via the occasional phone call or letter, their lives had barely touched. There was so much her aunt didn't know. And because Helene was sleeping off the effects of last night's binge and the resulting aftermath, when she'd thrown her sister's offering of a mug of sweet cocoa—'To help you settle, dear'—at the sitting-room wall then had hysterics, Bianca and Jeanne could at least have a frank and full discussion.

'I only met my father once. I was twelve,' Bianca explained. 'It was New Year's Eve and he was visiting London—he was living in the States at that time. He wanted to see me—he'd never shown an atom of interest before. I went to his hotel hating him, not because he'd never so much as acknowledged my existence, but because of what he'd done to my mother.'

She leaned back in her chair, remembering that dreadful day. 'A week before, something had gone wrong for Helene—don't ask me what, I can't remember—but she'd started drinking and getting maudlin and told me I was old enough to be told what a louse my father was.

'She was twenty-one when she met and married him. For two years she was blissfully happy, living the high life, and then she suspected he was seeing someone else. So she deliberately got pregnant with me, thinking that would stop him straying. But it didn't work. He left her for the latest sex symbol on the social scene. As part of the divorce settlement he bought a twenty-five-year lease on this house. And that was that; she never saw him again. I think she had loved him desperately, and never really got over it.'

Bianca shrugged, knowing she was probably about to shock her ultra-respectable aunt. 'I grew up in the changing company of a variety of "uncles". She could have married any one of them—they always seemed to be besotted. But there was always something wrong with them—in a nutshell they weren't Conrad Jay. She never stopped loving him but she needed these men in her life to convince herself that she was still desirable, worth something.'

She pulled a wry face. 'So there was I, twelve years old and hating my father, when that surprise phone call came through. Helene put me in a taxi to the hotel and my father put me in another to take me home.

'In between I told him exactly what I thought of him for the way he'd hurt my mother and said that under no circumstances would I ever agree to see him again. All this in front of his latest new wife. She couldn't have been more than seven or eight years older than me. So perhaps you understand why he is the last person I would ever appeal to for help. I have no idea how to contact him, even if I wanted to. And the moral of this story is something Helene once said to me—never marry a rich man. They know the price of everything and the value of nothing.'

Advice which had stuck more firmly than she'd realised, cemented in place by the damage such a marriage had done to her mother, the years of coping with the after-effects. Advice which had stood her in good stead when Cesare had made that shock offer of marriage.

Pushing him and what he had come to mean to her roughly out of her head, Bianca rose from the table and forced herself to think instead of how to handle the problem of helping Helene and holding down the job that was essential if she were to provide for them both.

Right at this moment it seemed completely impossible.

CHAPTER THREE

HE HAD her!

Had her exactly where he wanted her!

Cesare slid the sleek black Ferrari into a fortuitously vacant kerbside slot in front of the Hampstead house and switched off the ignition, the iron fist of inner harshness crushing that gut-punch of triumph, hardening his icy resolve.

His mouth flattened into a line of grim determination. Whatever the beautiful minx thought, he hadn't finished with Bianca Jay yet, not by a mile. The information he had at his fingertips would ensure that, until he said it was over, their affair would continue. On his terms this time, not hers. His Italian pride demanded it.

She would be taught that no woman brushed an Andriotti male aside as if he were of no more importance than a fly! It was a salutary lesson he would take great pleasure in giving.

Flicking a glance at the façade of her home, he battened down the recurring upsurge of anger with steely control. Don't get mad, get even, he reminded himself. Her carefully hoarded secrets were his now and he would use every last one of them to his own advantage.

Exiting the car, he activated the top-of-the-range security system, his mouth hard and flat as he mounted the steps and pressed the doorbell.

Yesterday's phone call to her boss, Stazia Lynley, had elicited the information that she had just received a surprise call from Bianca herself, requesting an indefinite period of unpaid leave, so unless she was in the habit of going shopping at eight in the morning she would answer the summons.

His loins kicked and hardened at the mere thought of seeing her again, of drowning in the witchery of her beautiful amber eyes, in the special just-for-him look of steamy sultriness that swamped the glorious, glowing depths when they lay together in tangled sheets. Two eager bodies, hours of mind-melting passion, melding her physically to him. Yet keeping her just out of reach, he reminded himself. Because he'd never known the truth of her; the real Bianca Jay had been carefully kept from him.

Until now.

Switching off lust was far harder than blocking out anger, he conceded edgily as he pressed his thumb against the bell-push again and kept it there. But by the time he heard the rasp of the bolts being drawn back his face was as bland as a slashing bone structure, a blade of a nose and a passionate mouth could ever hope to be.

'Cesare—' His name on the lushness of her lips was a falling sigh, as if seeing him here was more than she could hope to cope with, and as the quick flush of telltale and immediate colour receded he noted that her skin was ashy pale, her eyes dark-circled as if she's spent the past night in wakeful worry.

He hated to see that, although he knew he shouldn't. Compassion shouldn't come into the equation in his dealings with the witch who had taken his ego and stamped on it. Why should she sleep easily when he'd lain awake all night, alternately plotting revenge or consumed with anger and damaged pride?

Impatiently consoling the stubborn part of himself that felt pain at her distress with the knowledge that her anxiety over her mother would soon be ended, and quelling the stab of guilt over having brought her from her bed—as evidenced by the rumpled state of her long, silky black hair, the robe hastily flung on and belted over her naked body—he responded coolly, 'We need to talk.'

'There's nothing to say.' Her voice was wary and the hand that gripped the edge of the partly open door was white-knuckled. Her heart had leapt into her throat and was staying there, beating fast enough to choke her.

She had never thought to see him again, truly believing that having been told their affair was over he would watch her walk away with little or no regret, shrug his impressive shoulders and begin the process of finding the next willing candidate to share his night-time activities. It was the sort of thing men like him did.

Eyes that had been downcast since that first split

second of recognition now flicked wide to meet his
head-on. And as that familiar hot excitement perme-
ated her bloodstream she wished she'd kept her eyes
firmly on the floor.

Clad in a perfectly tailored light silky grey suit, the
crisp white shirt emphasising the olive tones of his
skin and the tough, shadowed jawline that was always
dark no matter how often he shaved, the dark charcoal
of his tie that matched the broody, moody colour of
his eyes, he looked exactly what he was—all-
sophisticated Italian male, king of the heap, effortlessly in total command of who he was, what he did.

Bianca sucked in a sharp, much-needed gulp of air.
The incredible impact of him had hit her with the usual
enervating body-blow, making it impossible for her to
do anything to deny him entry when he calmly walked
past her into the hall.

'Where?' he asked succinctly, his narrowed eyes
watching her with immovable cool, one dark brow el-
evating slightly to emphasise his question.

Wordlessly, every inch of her skin quivering beneath the covering of soft dove-grey satin, Bianca led
the way to the sitting room at the back of the tall,
narrow house, her mind flittering like an intoxicated
gnat as she sought reasons for his presence.

To call her names because she'd ended their affair
before he'd had time to grow bored with the relationship? That didn't seem in character. To him and many
other men in his position affairs such as theirs had
been were ephemeral and easily forgotten.

To beg her to return to him, or to repeat his crazy proposal of marriage? Both seemed unlikely. His Italian pride wouldn't let him beg.

But if he did, her tired mind panicked, would she be able to resist when she only had to look at him to be swamped by this incredible need?

She really didn't want this, her weary brain shrieked in protest. To see Cesare again was more than she could handle on top of everything else.

Her boss hadn't been one bit pleased at her inability to put a time limit on the amount of leave she needed. It was impossible to say how long it would take to find alternative, affordable accommodation and organise the move, somehow persuade a stubborn Helene to seek medical help, convince Jeanne that her presence was essential for a while longer.

Closing the sitting room door behind them, Bianca gave him what she hoped would pass as a look of impatience, desperately trying to keep the revealing mute misery from her eyes.

Cesare Andriotti should have looked out of place, his potent masculinity at odds with Helene's choice of ultra-feminine decor. But, as always, she thought with grudging admiration, he took control, his surroundings fading into insignificance before the force field of his commanding personality as he gestured her to one of the pair of delicate Edwardian chairs flanking a rose-wood tripod table in the window embrasure, before taking his time about seating himself.

His long legs loosely crossed at the ankles, his arms

resting on the delicate rosewood supports, his dark
head tipped back against the high, velvet-upholstered
back of the chair, he looked totally relaxed, only the
cold, brilliant glitter of his eyes telling her that, whatever his reason for being here, he meant business.

The silence sizzled with sexual tension, with the
stinging expectation of she knew not what. The way
he was looking at her now was doing her head in, his
incredibly sexy, moody eyes sliding over her as if he
was assessing every curve, line and hollow of her
lightly clad body, awarding her desirability points out
of ten.

Biting her lip, she managed thickly, 'What do you
want, Cesare?' And in a last-ditch attempt to stamp
some of her own authority on this unlooked-for meeting, she added, 'I honestly don't have much time; I've
a lot to get through today.'

And watched her words misfire as he ignored her
pathetic attempt to take control and listed smoothly,
'Your lease runs out shortly and on your salary I doubt
you can afford to renew it. Therefore the need to find
alternative accommodation is imperative. Not easy,
not when one considers the price of property in
London, and Helene Sinclair's liking for the luxuries
of this life.' He steepled his fingers, the tips resting
against the sensual curve of his lower lip. 'Am I not
right?'

Gazing at him speechlessly, Bianca felt what little
colour she did have drain out of her face. How did he
know her mother's maiden name? Who could have

told him that the twenty-five-year lease that had been part of her mother's divorce settlement was coming to an end?

She had been so careful to keep her personal life, her worries and concerns, out of their relationship. Not because she was ashamed of what her mother was rapidly becoming—falling in love with a wealthy sophisticate who thought it was his right to change his wives as often as he changed his cars had been to blame for the mess Helene was making of her life—but because opening up to Cesare would have made her even more vulnerable than she had been where he was concerned.

Besides, he wouldn't have been interested in her problems. Theirs had been the sort of affair he was used to, with both partners keeping to the ground rules. No strings, no commitment and certainly no messy soul-baring to bore the socks off him.

Unaffected by her silence, he continued remorselessly, 'A sought-after and very lovely model in her late teens and early twenties, your mother became used to admiring attention and the rewards of a big salary.'

He tilted her a look that told her he was amused by the way her mouth had fallen open with horrified disbelief at what she was hearing. 'Of course,' he opined smoothly, 'after her marriage to your father she would have become used to a life of idle luxury, the glitter and glamour of the international social scene, where all she had to do was look beautiful and collect the homage of enchanted males. After the divorce,' he continued with chilling silkiness, 'she'd long since lost the work ethic. But that didn't matter, did it? There was a substantial settlement.

'However—' his eyes impaled her, a helpless prisoner of his verbal torture '—the money drained away. Spent on wild parties, her racketty friends, the endless search for flattery. The excesses worsening during the last few months—places she was discreetly barred from and those she was rather too publicly thrown out of. Helene has more than a few problems.'

Again the infuriating upward drift of one eloquent brow. 'Need I say more?'

Shaking with shock, everything she'd kept from him out in the open, she felt desperately nauseous. He was gloating over her problems, he just had to be, and in that moment she hated him with a violence that threatened to shatter her completely.

Was this—this utterly hateful gloating—his way of getting back at her for ending their affair, for having the temerity to ignore his dangerously tempting, shock proposal of marriage?

Her body held immobile by the weight of his knowledge, her lips moved with awkward stiffness as she forced out, 'How the hell do you know all this?'

'Simple.' He had the gall to smile; the slow curving of his passionate mouth that had once had the power to enslave her now filled her with a wave of disgust that sent shivers shuddering down her spine. 'Through a private investigator. Blakely's the head of his sphere. A phone call, a name, an address, and he came up with a wad of interesting information.'

Anger brought her spine to attention, thrusting her breasts tight against the silky fabric. Flushing, she saw his gaze drop, fastening on the pouting globes, lingering, exactly like a caress.

Determinedly ignoring the way her skin fluttered, the sudden and definitely unwanted pooling of heat at the juncture of her thighs, she said as frostily as she could manage, 'Well, bully for you! Though I can't imagine what satisfaction you could hope to gain from digging the dirt on my family.'

'No?' His smile was pure menace.

Bianca had heard it said that Cesare Andriotti was the most ruthless bargainer on the planet. She had never seen that side of him before, and now that she had she felt her blood run cold. And her mouth trembled as she listened to the slow, self-assured pace of his next words.

'I get complete satisfaction. Does that answer your question? You see, *cara mia*, I have not yet grown tired of our affair, and until I'm sated—*I*, not you—it will continue.'

'No!' The instinctive and vehement repudiation was wrested from her. It wasn't going to happen! With each day that had passed she had fallen more and more in love with him. Ending their affair had been the hardest thing she'd ever had to do. To continue with it until he decided to say goodbye and move on would do even more damage to her already battered heart.

'In return—' he deliberately ignored the sheer anguish of that single word, steeling himself to discount the wretchedness in her golden eyes, eyes that had once glowed with incandescent pleasure on seeing him '—in return I will make your problems go away. I have already spoken to Professor Vaccari. Marco is an expert in the field of the addictive personality and he has agreed to give Helene the counselling she so obviously needs. Also, I will renew the lease on this property so that after two or three months on the island a fit and balanced Helene will have a home to return to.'

'You can't!' Her head was spinning so wildly it was all she could think to say. Even a short-term lease would cost many thousands. It was unthinkable—

'On the contrary.' His dark eyes slid to the way she was clutching the arms of her chair, her fingers white with the pressure she was exerting, as if she was desperate to find something real and solid to cling onto. 'I can do what I want to do. Before, when you shared my bed so willingly, you went against what I wanted. You refused to move in with me, refused my gifts.'

His lips pulled back against his teeth as he remembered. He'd seen her refusals as statements of independence, of distance, and he could barely admit, even to himself, how they'd hurt, how he'd experienced a crazy sense of loneliness. Ridiculous, of course.

'You can refuse again, naturally. That is your choice. But think about it for a moment,' he slid in when her eyes widened as they winged to his. 'Your problems will remain. And do you honestly think

Helene will go to her GP and ask for the help she needs? Or isn't her well-being your first priority?'

Of course it was! How dared he imply otherwise? She loved her mother and felt deeply sorry for her, understanding only too well what had made her the woman she was. Suddenly her eyes stung with tears and she blinked furiously and gritted her teeth to stop her mouth trembling.

Watching her, Cesare felt an iron band tighten around his heart. Was she stubborn enough, so determined to keep him out of her life, that she would refuse to consider his offer?

Was he, for the first time in his life, about to be denied something he'd set his mind on having? The thought that he might lose what he most wanted— Bianca Jay in his life and in his bed for as long as he wanted her there—gave him a hitherto unknown sensation of panic.

He rigorously quelled the feeling he refused to admit to, and his voice was silkily seductive as he brushed his own emotions aside and worked on hers with the skill of a master. 'Think of an island in the sun, a beautiful villa, expert professional care for Helene. You and I together, staying close by. And we're good together, you know we are. Keeping your part of the bargain shouldn't be too much of a problem.'

But it would! He could have no idea how big the problem would be!

It was almost too tempting. To be where she most

longed to be, a longing that went far beyond the wonder of feeling the length of his body against the arching eagerness of hers, skin against skin, mouth against mouth, a longing that went so much further, encompassing a need to be loved, a need for the total commitment he obviously couldn't or wouldn't give.

Unconsciously she shook her head. That deep longing belonged in the past. She couldn't want to be loved by a man who would use blackmail to get what he wanted. She wasn't that crazy, was she? Gathering her wandering thoughts, she forced herself to return to what he had said.

'You talk about an island, about treatment. Where? For how long?'

She knew her voice sounded flat. Deliberately speaking in a careful monotone was the only way to stop herself railing at the man who had been her lover and who now came in the guise of an enemy. For only an enemy could make demands that would leave her heart in ruins. 'And how do I know this professor whatever-his-name-is could help my mother?'

It all sounded too far-fetched to be believable. He was playing cruel games, he simply had to be, and how could she ever have imagined herself sinking fathoms deep in love with a man who would stoop to such measures? Nervous energy suddenly coursing through her, Bianca got to her feet and fled to the door, flinging it open. 'Please go.'

Cesare didn't move, but his eyes followed her every enticingly fluid movement.

She was angry now, sensationally so, her head flung proudly back on her slender neck, her glorious hair a dark and silky tangle, her eyes flashing amber warnings, her fabulous body taut, every curve lovingly highlighted by the sheen of her flimsy robe. His heart jumped in his chest and his body hardened. He had never wanted her as much as he did at this moment.

He ached to take her in his arms, rediscover every inch of her with hot masculine pleasure, to kiss her until neither of them knew where they were, to stamp his brand of ownership on her until she took back the icy statement she'd made on the night of Claudia's birthday dinner.

It took a supreme act of will-power to get the wayward instincts of his body back under control and an act of cool determination to regain mastery of the situation. Levering himself slowly to his feet, he leant back against the delicate table, his legs crossed at the ankles, his hands deep in his pockets, facing her across the length of the room.

'In answer to your questions, Professor Vaccari is the best there is. I would not have retained his services for an unspecified length of time had that not been the case. And my island is off the coast of Sicily—a few acres only, but beautiful. The villa will supply all the luxury Helene could want, with the added benefit of being isolated from the temptations of the dubious pleasures of city nightlife. Helene will receive expert and sympathetic counselling, on that you have my word. You and I will be close at hand. You will see her every day to judge her progress back to full health and ensure that she doesn't feel entirely cut off amongst strangers. And you will come to my bed whenever I call,' he taunted softly.

Bianca ground her teeth together until her jaw ached. She was seeing a side of Cesare Andriotti she didn't like at all, a side she had never guessed at during the time she had been slowly but only too surely falling in love with him. Arrogance was too tame a word to describe the way he was backing her into a corner.

Dimly aware of the sound of movement in the main body of the house, the aroma of coffee and toast that meant Jeanne was up and about and making breakfast, she closed the door. Expecting him to take his marching orders had been a futile exercise, and one she was deeply regretting now. It made her look a complete loser.

But she wasn't a loser, or not completely. She jerked her chin up, levelling him an icy glance down the short length of her elegant nose. 'To pay for Helene's treatment I spend my nights in your bed,' she stated grimly. 'It seems small recompense for the amount of hard cash you'll be laying out. Do you think you can just dig into the bottomless Andriotti coffers and buy what you want?'

His eyes gleamed darkly. *Dio*, he had never paid for a woman in his life, but he would willingly bankrupt himself for this woman to avenge himself for the way she had so insultingly dismissed him from her life.

Drawling deliberately, he countered, 'It is what people do, I think. See commodities they want and go out and buy them.'

So she was a 'commodity' now, was she? she fulminated angrily, then felt her shoulders sag in a draining kind of despair because when it came right down to it that was all she'd ever been to him. Or ever could be. The only anomaly being, in her case, her outright refusal to accept the gifts—the 'payments'—he'd tried to lavish on her.

Wrapping her arms around her body, she leant back against the door, her eyes closing as she tried to find a way out of this humiliating nightmare. As far as Helene was concerned, what he was suggesting sounded ideal. A luxurious villa on an idyllic island, fresh air, sunshine and someone sympathetic and qualified to help her back to health, back to a sensibly constructive as opposed to a destructive lifestyle.

The only impossible downside would be having to share Cesare's bed. Not a problem in the past—even now she could feel her body's response to the memories of how it had been for them—but now being forced into compliance to his will, knowing she was being bought and paid for, a victim of his cruel games, waking every morning to wonder if today would be the day when he told her he had tired of her. Part of her hoping it would be, the other part wanting him to stay with her for ever.

But would sleeping with him for her mother's sake be a problem? her weary mind slotted in. Her past attempts to get her mother to see her GP had met with total failure. But an Italian island belonging to the wealthy Andriotti family, luxury on tap, a few sessions with the top man in his field would appeal to the part of her that was firmly stuck back in her heyday, the universally envied wife of a handsome millionaire. She would feel special and pampered, not just a number in a long NHS queue.

Cesare was still waiting for her response. She could feel his eyes on her, burning her skin. Crunch time, she thought, her insides giving a hollow lurch.

Laving her dry lips with the tip of her tongue, she lifted her eyes and bargained throatily, 'In principle you don't give me much choice, but I want to alter the terms. Aunt Jeanne goes with Helene and I move in with you, here in London, if that's what you want.' She paused for a fraught moment to clear the constriction in her throat. 'That way you won't have to be away from your work and neither will I. I can look for alternative accommodation and that means you won't have to lay out I don't know how many thousands on renewing the lease here.'

And that way, at least, she wouldn't feel so sullied, her job would be safe and she could flat-hunt without worrying about what Helene was getting up to. And as soon as he'd tired of her—and, given what little she knew of his track record, that wouldn't be too far in the future—she would at last be free of him.

The silence stretched for long moments; she could hear her own breathing, ragged and jumpy, the muted tick of the mantel clock. He didn't appear to have heard a word of what she'd said, his expression not altering by a flicker of an eyelash.

Until he smiled. Just a lazy curving of the corners of his mouth as he enunciated the single word, 'No.'

It was settled over breakfast. Jeanne, tracking her niece to the sitting room, had insisted 'her visitor' join them for the meal. And Cesare, as Bianca had known he would, charmed her aunt on side.

'It's exactly what my sister needs. I had thought Bianca and I could cope between us, but, frankly, we can't. And I could do with a holiday, too. I haven't had one since my husband died—it's really most generous, Mr Andriotti. Most.'

'Not at all, Jeanne.' Cesare, accepting his second cup of coffee after appreciatively working his way through half a grapefruit, poached eggs followed by toast and honey, gave her the kind of smile that would turn any woman to mush. 'Bianca and I have been close friends for quite some time. If a friend of mine needs help, then I'm only too happy to do what I can.'

And not a single word about what his 'close friend' was going to have to do to secure this wonderful and so generous solution to Helene's little problem! Bianca pushed her untouched plate of toast away with huff worthy of a spoiled brat and unguardedly met his eyes.

Sexy eyes. Her insides looped the loop even while the palm of her hand itched to swipe that sardonically knowing smile off his handsome face, and she was saved from blurting out the truth and seeing Jeanne's grateful approbation turn to shocked outrage by Helene's entrance.

Mornings for Helene didn't normally begin before noon, and her early appearance must have been down to hearing a male voice, Bianca deduced, noting the full complement of warpaint, the obligatory ruffled, semi-transparent negligee.

Rising to pour her mother the strong black coffee that was all she ever took for breakfast, she abandoned Jeanne to perform the necessary introductions. Detecting the unmistakable smell of whisky on Helene's breath, Bianca mentally caved in.

She and Jeanne had systematically rid the house of alcohol, or so they'd thought. Helene must have a secret stash.

Defeat left her drained. She switched off and allowed the master of persuasion to use his considerable charm to make Helene see that a 'holiday' on a beautiful Italian island, with the undivided attention of a brilliant professor, was exactly what a woman of her sensitive nature needed.

Famous names—actresses, minor royalty, big-time sports personalities—were dropped like gilded hooks into the conversation. 'So many of the rich and famous often burn themselves out and owe their complete rejuvenation to Professor Vaccari' clinched the matter.

If Cesare Andriotti still classed her with the rich and famous, then that was more than fine by Helene Jay.

It made her feel just beautifully important, someone really special again.

Mutely, Bianca began to clear the breakfast dishes while Cesare said his goodbyes, promising to fax the details of their travel arrangements through during the next twenty-four hours. There was a hollow feeling inside her that had nothing to do with her inability to eat breakfast as she watched Helene flutter in his wake when she saw him to the door.

'I must get to the station and wait for the first train to Bristol,' Jeanne announced, her plain features pink with pleasure. 'It's bound to be much hotter on that island than it is here, so I must fetch some of my cooler things. I'll make sure I'm back later this evening. You can cope, can't you? She must have sneaked a bottle in—I could smell it on her.' The pink flush of pleasure deepened to condemnation. 'We can't get her to that professor person soon enough!'

A sentiment Bianca could only agree with, but the price would be cripplingly high. Annoyingly, her eyes swam with tears as she bent to load the dishwasher.

Cursing her mangled emotions, she furiously blinked the moisture away at Helene's approach, her amused, 'Who's a dark horse, then? I knew you were seeing someone—a girl doesn't creep in at dawn because she's been late-night shopping! But Cesare Andriotti, of all people! Darling,' she said quietly, sounding absolutely sober now, 'do be careful. He's gorgeous, charming and loaded and obviously a generous lover, so have a fling with him by all means, but don't fall in love with him. Been there, done that and it isn't worth the heartbreak.'

Tell me about it, Bianca thought grimly as Helene left the room, probably to finish what was left in that secret bottle.

The next few weeks—or as long as it took for Cesare to decide he'd tired of her—promised to be the worst of her life. Yet there was this feverish burning deep inside her when she thought of the coming nights, her part of the bargain, the way he could turn her into a wanton, wild thing with one touch, one explicit look from those sinfully moody, sexy eyes...

He had always been able to reach her on that level. From the first moment of her setting eyes on him their affair had seemed inevitable and, to her deep shame and regret, nothing he had done or said this morning had changed that.

CHAPTER FOUR

CESARE piloted the helicopter from Palermo on the final leg of the journey. Was there no end to this man's talents? Bianca thought sourly.

Helene, sitting up front, was indulging in non-stop, hyper chatter, too excited by the VIP treatment they'd received since leaving London in the Andriotti private jet to be pining for a drink. Yet.

In contrast, Jeanne was completely silent apart from the odd stifled moan, ferociously gripping the edges of her seat, her skin pale and delicately tinged with green, her eyes tightly closed.

Easy enough to explain away her own edgy silence by pretending to be similarly affected, Bianca reflected drearily, even if the way her stomach was churning had nothing to do with feeling airsick but was entirely down to the sublimely self-assured creature who was piloting the craft.

She put her fingers on the nape of her neck, vainly trying to ease some of the tension. Thankfully her hair was still securely anchored in its battery of pins, re-inforcing her intention to look as dowdy as possible—hence her lack of make-up, plain grey cotton trousers and unglamorous, shapeless T-shirt.

Helene, though, was dressed to kill. A brand-new

designer trouser suit in acid yellow—'Darling, I can't fly to Italy wearing any old rag!'—which had meant another heavy load on her credit card. A bill which she would have to pay, somehow, Bianca accepted tiredly. At the moment she wasn't earning and if Cesare stretched her punishment out into months instead of weeks she would lose her job for ever. Stazia wasn't noted for her patience. It didn't bear thinking about.

'My island.' Cesare's deep tones at last cut through Helene's chatter and Jeanne uttered a heartfelt groan as the machine dipped low over a green mound, fringed with pebbly beaches and surrounded by deep, translucent seas. 'The villa.'

They hovered, hawklike, over the white-walled, sprawling dwelling that appeared to be linked to a small natural harbour by a dusty white track.

Bianca heard Jeanne's squawk of terror as they plummeted towards the ground, and reached over to grasp her aunt's hand comfortingly, only slowly and with difficulty releasing the punishing grip when they landed gently and Cesare cut the engine.

The wait for the rotors to come to a standstill seemed interminable. Under any other circumstances, Bianca guessed sourly, Cesare would have exited long ago, his athletic body bending low to avoid the circling blades, in true macho fashion.

But mindful of the two middle-aged women in his care he was waiting. And talking. Explaining about the luxuries on tap, the villa's well of pure spring drinking water, the generator, the swimming pool, the full complement of staff who had arrived by boat the day before, Professor Vaccari who was already installed and waiting to meet them—on and on until Bianca wanted to hit him.

Her female relatives were hanging on his every word as if he were the most perfect thing ever to walk on two legs, Bianca noted on a fierce flare of acid frustration. They would rapidly change their minds if they knew they were only here, being treated like valued guests, because Cesare, the Wonder Man, wanted her in his bed until he decided he'd had enough of her!

But to see her mother cured of her dependence on alcohol, feverish shopping bouts and the need to be the centre of attention—no matter how demeaning—would be worth the sacrifice of her career and her self-respect, she staunchly reassured herself when at last they stood on the small plateau of grass with the arc of the almost impossibly blue sky above them and the whisper of the translucent sea on the rocky beach far below. But despite the warmth of the late afternoon sun she was shivering inside.

Deliberately keeping her eyes away from Cesare who, out of the sharp, beautifully cut business suits she was used to seeing him in, was now wearing stone-coloured combat trousers topped by an olive-green T-shirt and looking frighteningly hunky, she made herself take a painstaking and inordinate interest in the mule-drawn cart that was waiting to transport their luggage—the large bulk of it Helene's—up to the villa.

The mule wore a wide-brimmed straw hat. Holes had been cut in the brim to accommodate its long ears. The driver's name was Giovanni and he, too, wore a battered straw hat and when he grinned and said *'Buonasera'* she saw that his teeth were blackened stumps in his deeply tanned leathery face. She wondered if this wizened elderly man was a fixture on the island, employed to look after the villa, or whether he and his mule had been transported over from the mainland too.

Far easier to concentrate on the old man and the mule than watch the way the sunlight gilded Cesare's olive-toned skin and painted dark chestnut highlights onto his expensively barbered night-black hair.

'Come.' Cesare's voice, breaking into her thoughts, made her nerve ends splinter and the touch of his fingers as his hand cupped her elbow made her mouth run dry. If she closed her eyes she would see images of him, of his golden skin, of those long hands touching the smooth pale skin of her body, the smouldering desire in his smoky charcoal eyes as he lowered his head to kiss her.

Not only see the images that were indelibly printed on her brain, but feel them. Feel the burning heat of his skin against hers, the cataclysmic, mind-blowing magic of his kiss, the prelude to the sheer out-of-this world ecstasy of the heat and urgency of the shared climax of their love-making. Feel the way her heart blossomed with that growing and oh, so dangerous love for him.

A small, anguished groan left her lips as, unconsciously, she shook her head to chase away those unwanted mind pictures. Jerkily, she tried to move away from him, but his fingers tightened, and, as if he knew precisely what effect his close proximity was having on her, he sounded lightly amused as he pointed out, 'The track is not so steep. See, *cara mia*, the others have no difficulty. They will reach the villa long before us. So why don't you try to stop acting like a stubborn child, or do I have to carry you?'

Said with just the faintest touch of sarcasm. But inside his heart was thundering. He wanted to sweep her into his arms and kiss that sulky mouth into eager submission. Hear those throaty little mews of pleasure that always sent him spiralling out of control and filled him with the primitive urge to possess her, to have her begging for him, and only him.

One look from those fabulous golden eyes would be all it took to jerk him out of the controlled mastery of the situation that had been his ever since she'd ended their affair, just one look—

But, her eyes firmly on the two figures ahead of them, ascending the dusty white track as it curved round the gentle green hillside, she now knew how she had to act to make him wish he'd never blackmailed her into continuing their affair and said frostily, 'Don't be ridiculous, Cesare. I don't need carrying and

I'm neither a child, nor stubborn. I'm simply bored with the situation I find myself in.'

She felt his simmering, impotent fury as she began to walk steadily up the track. Boredom didn't come into it, of course. In fact her nerves were skittering about all over the place, her heart pounding as if she'd just run a marathon. If her inspired tactics worked he would soon want to see the back of her. He wouldn't want a woman who yawned her head off, or began trimming her fingernails when he made love to her!

She'd ended their affair because she'd broken all the rules and found herself falling in love with him. It had been a bad feeling, making her feel lost and lonely, but there had been dignity in it. But now she was expected to be the sex slave of a man she didn't love at all, and had been mad to ever even think she did—as she repeatedly had to remind herself—and being a toy bought and paid for until he threw her away was so very much worse.

There was no dignity in that. All she could do in defence of what little pride that remained to her was try to make the situation as unpleasant and demeaning for him as it was for her!

Cesare watched her walk away in blistering silence. Fury beat at his brain. Turning abruptly, as if the very sight of her might make him erupt completely, he helped Giovanni load the last of the luggage into the cart, talking to him in their native language, his voice calm, melodious. But inside he was still seething.

So the thought of being his lover bored her, did it?

She had ended their affair because he *bored* her!

Dio! But he would teach her differently! By the time he decided to end it she would be begging him to let her stay, clinging, pleading, promising him the earth, moon and stars if only he would keep her with him. Or his name wasn't Cesare Gianluca Andriotti!

'It's all quite beautiful!' Helene enthused brittly. 'Don't you agree, darling?'

'Yes.' Bianca forced the response through lips that felt as thick and numb as planks. Maria, the house-keeper, had given them the guided tour of the villa. All Bianca could recall was cool marble floors, light airy rooms furnished with understated elegance, and now they were on a terrace overlooking a sweep of lawn that descended gently to a white-beached cove lapped by an azure sea.

Maria had brought a frosted jug of fruit juice to the table and Bianca knew she should drink some because she was feeling dehydrated, but her stomach was a tight knot of tension, her throat clenched and aching. Helene had looked at her glass as if it were poison and the glitter of her eyes told of her need for alcohol.

At least Professor Vaccari looked capable of han-dling her, Bianca thought, grasping at the only positive aspect of this foul situation. In his mid-fifties, at a guess, with close-cropped greying hair and the profile of a Roman senator, he had kind, clever eyes and an aura of calm competence.

He now rose from his seat and pressed a discreetly

placed bell-push on the wall behind him. 'Ladies, if you will—Maria will come and show you to your rooms. Giovanni has taken your luggage up and Rosa will have unpacked for you. We will meet here in one hour to dine.'

The professor's lightly accented voice was infused with gentle authority and Helene shot from her own seat with more alacrity than grace. If she'd hidden bottles of forbidden alcohol in her suitcases, then they would have been spirited away by Rosa on his instructions, Bianca guessed.

'Shall we go up then, darling?'

As Maria appeared Helene stretched out a hand to her daughter, her brows peaked with mute entreaty, but Cesare supplied incisively, 'Bianca and I will be staying elsewhere—a mere ten minutes' walk away.' He moved away from the terrace wall where he'd been a silent, brooding presence, obviously intent on allowing the professor to take charge of the proceedings, lead the conversation where he would.

Although she'd known what he'd intended Bianca felt the colour drain from her face as she faced the hateful and now immediate reality of her situation. The bargain he'd made was to remain their dark secret and if her mother were to benefit from her time here then she mustn't even suspect that her daughter was an unwilling partner in Cesare Andriotti's bed.

It cost her a lot to dredge up a smile, to disregard the sudden flare of maternal anxiety in Helene's eyes and say, 'I'll see you every day. For lunch, maybe.'

This to let Cesare know that he couldn't dictate her every movement, bargain or no bargain. The carefully concocted lightness of her tone meant to allay her mother's fears. Fears that she would fall in love with the type of man her own husband had been.

On a sudden surge of emotion she rose to hug her mother, holding her close, her heart clenching painfully as she felt the frailty of the bony body beneath the brave new designer suit. The coming sessions with the professor had to work out, they simply had to!

In a choky voice, for Helene's ears only, she gave the needed reassurances. 'You'll be fine. Just fine. Honestly you will. Just concentrate on getting well and happy. And I'm not going to get emotionally involved with Cesare, believe me. So don't worry about me—promise?'

The mute nod of her mother's head was all she needed. With the promise, 'I'll see you some time tomorrow,' Bianca turned away, her eyes bright with the tears she was desperately trying to hold back, and met the dark, unreadable intensity of Cesare's gaze.

Her chin came up. If he thought she was playing to the gallery, behaving with mawkish sentimentality, then so be it. Why should she care what he thought of her? All that mattered was Helene's well-being. Meeting his eyes with a look meant to convey withering scorn, she stated, 'We'll make ourselves scarce, shall we?'

Cesare's perfect body stiffened slightly and a dull flush of anger stained his angular cheekbones. *Dio*, but she was getting to him! Showing him the lamb wouldn't go willingly to the slaughter! And watching her fold Helene in that loving embrace had made him feel bad about himself for the first time in his life. It was not something he was comfortable with.

Making a tight gesture towards the flight of steps that led down from the terrace he said through his teeth, 'Down there. Wait for me.' Then he turned to watch Helene and Jeanne follow Maria back into the house, exchanging a few words with his old friend Vaccari while he got rid of the startling and shameful need to turn Bianca over his knee and paddle her delectable backside.

The thought of using physical violence against a woman was utterly abhorrent to him and had never before entered his head. He didn't know what was happening to him, or why this one woman should arouse such intense and warring emotions in him.

The silent ten-minute walk took them over the brow of the hill that sheltered the villa from the storms that could come out of nowhere and down the other side to a cup-shaped valley.

In any other circumstances Bianca would have found the experience full of delights, from the wild-flower-strewn grass at her feet, the scent of wild herbs on the still, warm air, the magical views of one or two of the other distant volcanic islands in the Aeolian group that seemed to float like misty smudges on the azure sea. But she might just as well be walking on a

London back street, in the rain and in the dark, for all the pleasure the surroundings gave her.

Even though her hastily formed plan seemed to be working—her idea of making it plain that she viewed the continuation of their affair as nothing more than a boring chore—the tension was getting to her, a tight, spiralling knot deep inside her that threatened to unwind with explosive consequences at any moment.

Despite the slightly cooler air as the sun dipped towards the misty horizon, perspiration was sticking her clothes to her body, beading on her forehead and on the nape of her neck. Cesare hadn't attempted to touch her, hadn't spoken a single word, his obvious and brooding anger telling her her tactics were working. All she had to do was keep them up.

It was a scary feeling.

Her heart stopped and then raced on at redoubled speed when they suddenly reached their destination. The little stone-built house, half hidden by a slab of volcanic rock, sat in the sea of ferns that bordered a dancing crystal stream and looked idyllic, the perfect lovers' hideaway.

Reminding herself that there was nothing perfect about the situation, Bianca swallowed the stubborn pride that had made her match his silence and asked stiltedly, 'What is this place?' because somebody, at some point, had to say something!

Pausing in the act of pushing open the hewn plank door, Cesare gave her a grim smile. 'Our love-nest?'

He raised one sable brow interrogatively, then answered his own question drily. 'Perhaps not.'

The thick dark sweep of his lashes hid his expression and Bianca gave him a frigid stare, lifting her slender shoulders in a throwaway shrug. There was no 'perhaps' about it. Love had never entered their relationship except on her part. And how could a sane woman love such a monster?

'To be entirely factual—' his mouth curved, as if her glare had amused him but only very slightly '—the former owner of the island lived here until he died. He was what you might call a recluse, working a small patch of land to grow capers and a few vines, fishing, harvesting the wild rosemary, making a living for himself. Now it is used as overspill accommodation for the extra staff needed when the family and their friends use the villa for autumn holidays.' He stood aside for her to enter, his tone clipped when he asked, 'Curiosity satisfied?'

Bianca didn't answer. There was no way she could make the attempt when there was a lump the size of Gibraltar in her throat. She stepped over the threshold, lowering her head to hide the incipient tears from his gaze.

Stupid to mourn what had been, the joy they'd found in each other, the way he'd turned on that fabled charm, flirting with her, the million and one things they'd talked about, the million and one ways they'd found to pleasure each other, the touch of his hand, the look in his eyes that had told her he'd wanted her, had found her beautiful.

Stupid to mourn what had never been real. In any case, it was over. Any tender feelings she'd had for him had died when he'd thrown blackmail at her. So why did she feel as if part of her had died, too?

Stupid!

Cesare pulled in a long breath, watching her narrowly as her eyes swept the long, low-ceilinged room that lay beyond the old plank door, simply furnished with a Calor gas stove, stone sink, table, chairs and chunky wooden cupboards.

The nondescript clothes she'd chosen to travel in did nothing to hide the enticing curves of her slender body, or to render her movements any the less graceful. And the scraped-back style of her hair today merely emphasised the slim vulnerability of the achingly beautiful lines of her neck and throat.

Bunching his hands into fists, he swallowed a despairing oath. He didn't want it to be like this; this spiky stand-off was the last thing he wanted! He wanted it all back again, just as it had been—to see her smile, her lips curving sometimes with her slightly offbeat humour, or slowly, enticingly, seducing him with promises of sheer heaven. He wanted to see her eyes sparkle for him across a candlelit dinner table, to touch her hand, fingers instinctively interlacing, and know that before the night was out they would be stripping the clothes from each other's eager bodies.

His entire body clenched as she slowly reached out

to gently touch the petals of the wild flowers in an earthenware bowl in the centre of the solid wood table, placed there, no doubt, by whichever of the staff had readied the old stone house for occupation. The cheerful beauty of the blossoms seemed inappropriate—a bunch of thistles would have been more apt!

He ached to hold her in his arms, to feel those soft curves melt into the hardness of his body. Already he could feel his breathing thicken, the muscles surrounding his manhood tighten.

Gritting his teeth, he ignored the certainty that he could make her eat her words, admit that their lovemaking didn't bore her—*Dio*, but he knew her body so well, knew exactly how to touch her, where to stroke, where to kiss, where to suckle, until she became a writhing, slick, furnace of passion...

But he didn't want that. Not just sex. Suddenly, inexplicably, he wanted more.

His body urged him forward, every muscle and sinew straining to take what he knew could be his while his brain wrestled with this new conundrum, trying to write it off as nonsense, telling him that he'd be taking a step into the unknown if he stuck to the fantasy of wanting more from this one woman than he'd ever imagined he could need.

'It's not up to the standard of the villa.' His voice sounded grim as he broke the silence, but he couldn't help that. 'I'm afraid you'll just have to do without life's pleasant luxuries.' He knew the comment was unfair. Bianca was the least pampered and avaricious woman he had ever known, but something inside him prompted him to lash out, even though he despised himself for it.

He might not have spoken, only the faint tremor of her hand as she drew it back from the flowers told him she had heard every word and was probably, and rightly so, treating them with the contempt they deserved.

Expelling a short breath, he told her shortly, 'Take a look around. Get acclimatised while I check out the generator,' then turned his back on her and strode back through the door.

Outside, he sank onto a wooden bench, his long legs outstretched, his head tilted back against the rough, sun-warmed stones of the wall.

The generator would be fine. His staff were paid well to ensure that everything on the island ran like well-oiled clockwork. He'd simply needed any excuse to put space between them, to try to sort out what was going on inside his head.

That sudden and bewildering need to build something stronger and more enduring with a woman than sex and a transitory pleasure in her company he viewed with scepticism. It had never happened before and was only happening now, he analysed, because she'd put a huge hole in his pride, a hole that needed to be filled by her complete and utter compliance. Not only in bed, but something more—wresting from her the final submission. Love. Commitment. Eternal togetherness.

Once he had that his pride would be satisfied.

His mouth curled down on that degrading thought. It was unworthy, contemptible. He dismissed it. His pride would have to learn to live with a gaping hole.

Springing to his feet, he raked his fingers through his hair. His initial plan was cancelled. It wouldn't work. Forcing her to share his bed until he called it a day had been the cruellest, most insane idea he'd ever had. He couldn't now imagine how he'd ever come up with it in the first place.

What if the dangerous plan turned round and bit him, if it was he who never wanted to call it a day? If he became the one who craved complete commitment?

Just thinking about it turned the whole idea of self, of who he was and what he wanted, on its head.

And sent a shaft of debilitating sensation clear through the length of his body.

He knew exactly what he had to do.

Helene's treatment, under the wise and expert guidance of Marco Vaccari, would stand. Not because it was part of the iniquitous bargain, but because Cesare genuinely wanted to help. If Bianca had problems he had to do what he could to lift them from her slender shoulders. And after a week, say, the time necessary to see her mother settled, Bianca would be free to return to London and her career, free to find another man to pleasure her until he, too, began to bore her.

That thought lanced through him like a sharp-edged burning sword. Breathing deeply to control and con-

quer the searing pain of unaccustomed jealousy, he
lifted his chin and re-entered the house.

And called her name.

The devilish game was over.

CHAPTER FIVE

BIANCA heard Cesare call her name and everything inside her immediately froze into a tense, waiting stillness and all she could hear in the following deep silence was the thunder of her heartbeats. Then a tight, sexually insistent sensation began down in the centre of her body, making the blood curl hotly through her veins and her breath come in shallow, tortured little gasps.

Was this it, then? Had the time come for her to keep her part of his cruel bargain? To submit, to wait for him to mount the stairs and come to her, strip the clothes from her already shamefully sensitised body, to touch, caress, to plunder?

Did he know, damn him, that she only had to think about those clever hands of his on her body to be more than eager to submit to anything he wanted, a willing wanton, to burn and tremble for his touch, to feel the liquid heat pooling between her thighs?

Did he know that? Or was it her humiliating secret?

She'd been standing, wooden limbed, in the second of the two bedrooms. Both were identically furnished. Twin beds separated by a small night table, a chest, a large hanging cupboard.

Her suitcase was in here. There was no sign that

he'd brought anything with him, but the cupboard held clothes that she presumed were his. Casual trousers, a pair of well-worn jeans, shirts in the softest, lightest cottons. She'd withstood the utterly ridiculous temptation to touch them, to hold them to her face, and had quickly closed the cupboard door to stare at the night table as if the innocuous piece of furniture were the most important thing in the universe.

Would he lift it out of the way, push the beds together, or would he take what he wanted from her and then move away, sleeping alone?

In the past, in the short time left to them after repeatedly and languorously making love, before she'd left him around dawn, they'd lain entwined together, not ready to relinquish the drugging sensation of skin on skin, flesh bound to flesh...

As Cesare called again Bianca pulled herself together. Fatal to allow him to come and find her. He might think she was actually inviting...

Her mouth dry, her heart pounding, she plunged from the room and down the short flight of stairs to find him doing nothing more threatening than placing a pan of water on the stove. Crunch time seemed to have been delayed. Desperately, she moistened her lips with the tip of her tongue, willing her wretched knees to stop shaking.

Her only defence against the power of his attraction, the destructive, needy pulse of her flesh, was to act as if she viewed this enforced togetherness with bored resignation. But how to manage that when he could make her pulses sing with just one look from those sultry, wickedly sexy dark eyes?

'Ah, there you are.' He didn't look at her, simply adjusted the burner beneath the pan and added salt from a terracotta pot. 'I'm making an early supper.' He turned then, his hands on his narrow hips, the prosaic, unemotional words that would give her her freedom dying on his lips in the face of what he was seeing.

Dio, but she looked done in, her skin pale, almost ashen, those glorious eyes full of tension, her lush mouth tightened against too-revealing tremors, her rigid pose definitely defensive.

His heart clenched with compassion. He had done this to her and he hated himself for it. He said softly, his voice thickening in his throat, 'Why don't you take a shower while I cook? No bath, I'm afraid—I know you prefer it—but we need to conserve water.'

And still she stood there, as if frozen to the spot. He watched a shiver flutter over the exposed skin of the forearms that were protectively crossed about her body, saw the resulting goosebumps. It made him feel sickeningly guilty and it took all his will-power to put a stop to the instinctive need to close the small distance between them, to hold her, comfort her, apologise for forcing her into this situation.

But one touch would be a touch too many. He knew he would inevitably give way to the primitive urge to kiss her senseless, reclaim the magic of everything they had once had.

No way could he let himself do that because there was something different here, something deeper. Never during their time together had the need to offer comfort arisen. They had been equals, neither of them asking or needing anything from the other apart from an uncomplicated pleasure in each other's company and great sex. Superficial, definitely, but what they had both wanted, surely?

There was nothing superficial about what was going on in his mind right now. It was deep, it was tortuous, and he damned well didn't understand it.

'Go. Supper in fifteen minutes.' It cost a lot to smile, find a light tone of voice that didn't betray his inner turmoil, but it was worth it. She flinched, jerked herself out of her trancelike state and headed back towards the stairs.

The small bathroom was basic but scrupulously clean and the needles of warm water went some way towards easing the tension from her bones.

Wrapping herself in a fluffy white towel, Bianca headed back to the bedroom they were obviously meant to share, opening her suitcase and scanning the contents, eventually plucking out a fresh pair of jeans, old and worn to a comfortable softness, and a work-manlike plain dull green shirt.

Defensive dressing, she recognised wryly. And boy, did she need it! The smile he'd given her when he'd told her she had fifteen minutes before supper was ready had filled her with a flurry of confusion. It was

as if she had the old Cesare back, the perfect, consid-
erate lover whose touch she had craved with a desperation beyond reason. It had taken a whole load of
will-power to stop herself bursting into ridiculously
feeble tears and asking if they could please, please, go
back to the way they had been.

A foolish, demeaning and dangerous course. She
wouldn't let herself end up like her mother, a rich
man's trophy, easily won and just as easily discarded.
Ending up broken in heart and spirit.

Suitably armoured, her hair hanging down past her
shoulders in damp, decidedly unglamorous tendrils,
Bianca made her way downstairs, her nose twitching
at the aroma of garlic.

There was a bowl of salad on the table, a bottle of
wine, two glasses, and he was ladling the contents of
the pan onto two plates as she stepped through the
door. Pasta with an olive oil and garlic dressing, sprin-
kled with pecorino cheese.

Bianca's stomach gave a hungry gurgle and
Cesare's mouth twitched.

'Dig in. If you're as hungry as I am you won't want
to stand on ceremony.' Cesare smiled for her, spoke
lightly as he pulled out a chair for her and poured
gutsy Sicilian red wine into two glasses.

Thankfully matching his mood, Bianca smiled right
back at him. She could afford to relax for just a short
while, couldn't she? Go with the flow until it was time
to put up her guard again and handle him as she would
handle any enemy. The state her nerves were in she

owed herself that much, didn't she? And no way would she let herself be trapped into his web of seduction if that was what this new, smoother mood was all about.

If he insisted she share his bed—as was his stated intention—then she would force herself to be as responsive as a plank of wood. And maybe, as the *coup de grâce*, she would manufacture a coughing fit at the strategic moment!

But when that moment came wouldn't she be as lost in the wonder, the sheer sizzling excitement of what he could do to her, to do anything of the sort?

Firmly pushing that unnerving thought right to the back of her mind, she helped herself from the bowl of crisp green salad he handed her and opined as lightly as she was able, 'So we can add cooking to your list of no doubt endless accomplishments, can we?'

'Spaghetti is simple and about as much as I can manage with any hope of success. Fortunately, I know you like it.' That, and her preference for taking a bath rather than a shower, was the sum of his small knowledge of the essential woman.

He took a healthy swallow of his wine and leaned back in his chair, thoughtfully watching her as she ate. Before he handed her back her freedom and allowed her to leave his life, he would try to discover just what made her tick, find the real and lasting truth of Bianca Jay, the essence of her.

The rational part of his brain told him to forget it. Getting to know, really know, the woman who would soon have no part to play in his life would be an exercise in futility, but his heart said something else entirely. He would make the elusive, enticing, enigmatic little witch open up to him because on some level it was deeply important.

A shudder racked its way through the length of his body as he watched her raise her glass to her mouth. He wanted those lips on his, opening for him, warm for him, inviting the heady intimacies they had once so gloriously shared. He wanted her. He wanted her now!

But it couldn't happen. She had told him their affair was over and now he'd finally come to his senses he would let her go. But first, and gently—

'Bee—how badly did your father's desertion affect you?'

Bianca replaced her glass on the table and picked up her fork. She hadn't expected to be addressed by that fond diminutive and she hadn't expected that kind of question, but maybe she should have done. It seemed entirely logical. After all, he'd probably gone to a whole heap of expense to gain the background information she'd been so careful to keep from him. He just wanted to fill in the details, make sure he got his money's worth!

What had she got to lose, anyway? He'd already taken the most important things from her: her job, her self-respect. Besides, keeping him talking would delay the inevitable. Bed.

'Not at all,' she responded flatly, laying down her

fork instead. 'You don't miss what you never had. My father showed no interest in me, never wrote and asked for a photograph, not even when I was newborn, apparently. He did ask to meet with me once,' she admitted with a telling, throwaway shrug of her narrow shoulders. 'I was twelve years old. The meeting was a disaster. I haven't seen or heard from him since.'

'But it affected Helene badly, didn't it?' Cesare lounged back in his seat, his veiled eyes taking in the way that last remark had made her stiffen her spine, firm her lush mouth. 'Some of what she was going through—is still going through, even after all these years—must have rubbed off on you.'

'Perhaps.' She conceded that point because it was the truth, but added tightly, 'Does it matter?'

'I think so.' She was back behind her self-protective wall and he was going to break it down, find the truth of the woman who had been his lover for what, with hindsight, had probably been the best six months of his life.

His line of reasoning would leave him open to a large and probably painful session of ego-bashing. But he could take it, he would have to if he wanted to know where she was coming from.

Pouring more wine for both of them, he verbalised his conclusions with a calmness that belied the internal knife-thrusts of regret. 'Because of Helene's inability to come to terms with the way her husband dumped her—possibly for someone younger, with longer legs, perter breasts and bigger hair—you are afraid of committing your emotions to any man. Especially the sort of man your father is—men who only have to snap their fingers and wave a gold-plated cheque-book around to get exactly what they want.'

Spot on! Well, bully for you! she fumed, hating the feeling of being under a microscope. This intrusion into her psyche was unwarranted. On his part their relationship had been, literally, skin-deep. Great sex had been all he'd ever asked for!

Refusing to give him the satisfaction of telling him his analysis was absolutely right, she picked up on the other point, her eyes clashing defiantly with his. 'As I recall, you never wanted emotional commitment. You'd have run a mile if you thought I wanted anything of the sort. So I don't know what you're complaining about.'

'Touché!' His dark eyes danced and his long, sensual mouth curved wryly and Bianca's heart kicked violently against her ribs.

The charismatic machismo that was so uniquely his flayed her, it really did. He only had to turn the smouldering power of those incredibly sexy charcoal eyes of his on her to bring her body to stinging, exhilarating life. And if he knew why she'd ended their affair—because she'd fallen fathoms deep in love with him—he'd laugh his socks off and then run that mile!

He looked totally at ease though, one arm relaxing over the back of his chair, the long fingers of one hand idling on the stem of his wineglass, so unconfrontational that his next remark shook her.

'So you use men. Stay around until you get bored. And then move on to the next lover.'

'Isn't that what you do?' she flung at him just as soon as she'd recovered the ability to speak at all. Pot calling the kettle black seemed an entirely apt cliché at this moment.

'There haven't been as many women in my life as you possibly imagine.'

Bianca took a reckless gulp of wine, then levelled at him, 'So that makes it all right, does it?'

Was it her imagination, or had all the bones in his face tightened with suppressed anger at her nasty little quip? She gave a little huff of scorn for her own foolishness. He had every right to think as he did. She'd been the one to end their affair and earlier today she'd as good as told him he bored her.

As an impression it was as far from the truth as it could possibly get, but it was the only one that could make him back off. No red-blooded male—and Cesare Andriotti was more red-blooded than most—would want a woman who gave the impression that she found it as exciting as a cup of cold tea to be sharing a bed with him.

And as if picking up on her train of thought he remarked coldly, 'You obviously love Helene, worry about her. So much so that you'd agree to continue to have sex with a man who apparently has started to bore you.'

So it was getting to him, was it? Well, that had been her intention, the only way to defend herself. And now

was the time to ram her message home, hurt that
Italian pride of his, dent it so badly that he would
never, ever, want to touch her again.

'If I was backed in a corner and had no other option,' she agreed just as coldly. 'As you, of all people,
have every reason to know. And I'd even marry you,'
she taunted, deep, gut-twisting hurt making her voice
hard because she'd begun to want to be his wife, for
him to love her as she knew, deep down, she still loved
him. 'You did ask me, remember? Which, coming
from the man who told me—and really meant it—that
he enjoyed his bachelor freedom too much ever to fall
into that sort of trap, was a real eye-opener, believe
me! What did you have in mind? Tie me down legally
until your attention began to wander, if it was the only
way you could have me in bed?'

Cesare snapped to attention, a dull stain of colour
creeping over his cheekbones, his fists clenching until
his nails bit into his palms. The little witch was punching beneath the belt! He'd hoped her obvious uninter-
est in his proposal would have kept her off that par-
ticular embarrassing subject! And, *Dio*, but he didn't
know what his intention had been!

That offer of marriage had sprung out of nowhere,
certainly not from his reasoning mind, just as had his
plan for exacting revenge by way of blackmail—thus
going against every principle he'd ever held. Sprung
out of the driving and possibly insane need to keep
her with him at any cost!

He pushed his chair back from the table and was

on his feet at the very moment she did the same. He felt physically sick. He vented a savage oath in his own language, wishing to hell he knew what was going on here, why this one woman could get to him the way she did.

Watching through slitted eyes as she headed for the door, he asked grimly, 'Where are you going?'

'Out. Anywhere. Away from you!' she flung back at him as she dragged open the door. She just had to get away before she broke down entirely, weakly admitted that she hated the way things were between them now, confessed that she really despised herself for wanting to hurt him, that she loved him, warts and all, and then found herself promising to stay with him for just as long as he wanted her.

It was beginning to get dark as Bianca stumbled to the top of the grassy incline at the rear of the stone house, back the way they had come just an hour or two earlier. Now the sky was an arc of dusky amethyst, clearing to a band of aquamarine on the horizon where it dipped down to the misty sea.

Below her, not too far away, she could see the lights of the villa. It would be easy enough to make her way down there, ask—Maria, was it?—to find her a room for the night, fabricate some excuse for the request.

But it would be the coward's way out and she couldn't take it. This was between Cesare and herself and she had to think her way through it.

Turning her back on the beckoning lights, she walked slowly on until she came across a deep grassy hollow and sank down on the turf that still retained the heat of the sun.

Drawing her legs up, she looped her arms around them and laid her head against her knees, her hair falling like a dark curtain, cutting her off from everything but her jumpy thoughts. She sucked in a thick gulp of air, tasting the salt of her tears at the corners of her mouth.

Things couldn't go on this way, they simply couldn't. She couldn't keep her side of the devilish bargain; it would do too much damage. She still loved him, fool that she was, and making love with him, knowing that for him it was simply lust and a primitive need to punish her, waiting for him to wash his hands of her, would be like consigning herself to a nightmare that would have no ending.

A harsh sob racked her slender frame and she drew her elbows to her knees and pressed her fingertips as hard as she could against her tightly closed eyelids. Giving way to this swamping, absolute misery would get her nowhere. She knew what she had to do so there was no point in pretending she didn't.

It was unworthy of her to use the devious ploy of making him believe she'd finished their affair because he bored her. She had to come right out with it and tell him she refused to keep her side of the bargain. He might stoop to blackmail but he wouldn't stoop to rape!

And as for Helene, well, she would have to take her chances where her mother was concerned. Surely

Cesare wouldn't tell her to pack her bags and throw her off the island? He couldn't be that heartless.

In all the time she'd known him he'd never said a cruel word against another living soul, or dealt a cruel deed. Only towards her, and that only after she'd punctured his arrogant pride.

She wished she'd never met him!

She burst into tears.

His chest heaving from his exertions, his shirt sticking to his back, Cesare half ran, half slid down the steep grassy slope.

He'd panicked, he freely admitted, as he'd scoured the island, looking for her. The northern end first because there the cliffs were sheer, the edges crumbling. With Bianca alone, in the near dark, and not knowing the terrain, anything could have happened.

Panic had been pushing him on towards the villa to enlist Marco and Giovanni in the search when the heart-rending sound of a muffled sob had stopped him in his tracks, stopped his heart for an endless moment before it had hammered on.

The beam of his powerful torch had picked out her hiding place and the mixture of relief and remorse had made him light-headed.

A crouched bundle of sheer misery, she looked wounded, and as he reached her and drew her to her feet his only need was to comfort her.

Drawing her bowed head gently into the angle of his shoulder, he felt his heart swell with some wrench-

ing and nameless emotion. Then, feeling the fine tremors that shook her, he silently and savagely castigated
himself for what he had done to her.

Well, no more. No more demands. He would ask
nothing more of her, only that she find happiness.
'Bee, don't cry, I can't bear it,' he murmured raggedly.
Her hair was silky soft beneath his lips. He inhaled
deeply of her elusive, personal perfume and forced
himself not to react.

'I'm sorry,' he uttered thickly as the warmth of her
skin beneath her light clothing met the warmth of his
and started the usual minor conflagration that he knew
would quickly become spectacularly major if he didn't
do something about it.

Such as tell her she was free of him, of his unfair
demands. And tell her right now.

Sliding a not quite steady forefinger beneath her
chin, he made her lift her head and look at him and
recognise his sincerity, but the words died in his
throat, choking him, when the starlight illuminated the
golden, drowning depths of her utterly beautiful eyes,
the lush, slightly tremulous curves of her sinfully kiss-
able mouth.

'I—'

Bianca started to say something and immediately
and comprehensively forgot what it was.

The austere lines of his face mesmerised her; the
dark intensity of his eyes, shadowed by those amaz-
ingly thick lashes, melted her bones, made her so
stingingly aware of the heated pressure of the strong,

capable hands locked on either side of her waist, of the way their bodies were just touching, breast to thigh, of the tingle deep inside her that was rapidly becoming an insistent throb.

Incapable of moving away—as some distant only-just-functioning part of her brain told her she should—Bianca slid her hands to the wide span of his shoulders, her palms flat, and as her fingers curved instinctively into the tightly muscled structure she felt his chest expand with a rapid intake of breath just before his dark head dipped down, to take her lips with his hungry mouth.

CHAPTER SIX

BIANCA'S mouth welcomed his as eagerly and instinctively as it had ever done in the past, opening for him, tasting him, all her senses exploding in the glorious wonder of him and what he could make her feel.

Looping her arms around his neck as his hands strained her even closer in an urgency that spoke of desperate hunger, she became what she always had been for this one man: the original compliant female to the masterful, demanding male, parting her feet, the arch of her hips lifting, straining towards his hard male arousal in unspoken, willing invitation.

The harsh intake of his breath when he finally allowed their lips to separate sent a quiver of needle-sharp anticipation right down to the soles of Bianca's feet, and when his hands feverishly skimmed her body she groaned with pleasure and reached for him, kissing him again with a passion that sent her into orbit. Her last coherent thought was that it wasn't in her power to stop this happening.

With boneless accord they sank down to the soft, sweetly scented grass, clinging to each other wordlessly until he broke the kiss and uttered a spate of Italian endearments, adding thickly, 'Bee, I need you, I can't get enough of you!'

The strand of shocking, aching vulnerability in his husky voice nearly broke her heart. She, with her cowardly self-defence mechanism, had done this to him. Cesare really did believe he'd begun to bore her and the first wholly rational thought she'd had since he'd laid down his terms for the treatment Helene needed zipped through her brain with diamond-bright clarity.

She loved him far too much to see the personal pride that was so much a part of his charismatic persona brought down low. She simply couldn't bear it, she thought emotionally.

The need to give reassurance, the love she couldn't deny no matter how hard she tried, had her shaky fingers lifting the hem of his T-shirt to give her access to the hard, bronzed flesh beneath.

Touching the warm skin with the tips of her fingers, she felt his chest expand, heard the sharp intake of air and bent her head to lave one hard male nipple and then the other with the moistness of her tongue, the caressing exploration of her hands moving from the wide span of his shoulders to the arch of the ribcage that sheltered his heavily beating heart.

But when the palms of her hands slid over taut flat muscles and her fingers curled round the button on the waistband of the casual combat trousers his whole body went rigid as he stated through his teeth, 'You don't have to do this.'

His hands took her wrists in an iron grip but she could feel the trembling of his bones as he sought to control what she was doing to him. Her voice sultry,

Bianca told him, 'I do. I want to. You excite me. Why else would I be trying to seduce you?'

Then, her long hair lying like a silken cloud over his skin, she placed her lush mouth just above that disputed button, heard his muffled wrenching groan, his grip on her captive wrists slackening as he gave himself up to the waves of spiralling pleasure that obliterated his normally monumental will-power.

No other woman had ever been able to sap his will, no other woman had had this much power over him, was his last coherent thought as his whole world contracted into the small area of rocketing sensation and scorching expectancy, concentrating only on each tingling movement where the backs of her fingers brushed against his skin as she undid that button and then slowly, so very, very slowly, slid the zip down, exposing him to the softly warm night air, to her eyes, her hands, her mouth.

The delicate sensuality of her exploration made him shake, his spine arching, his breathing ragged and shallow, the exquisite pleasure she was giving him pushing him to the outer limits of control until, with an almost feral groan, he clamped his hands on either side of her bowed head and lifted her away, turning her pliant body until she lay beneath him.

He was taking control now and the little minx had been lying. Their love-making didn't bore her, she was as turned on as he was! He vented a soft, guttural cry of triumph before he took her mouth with scorching passion, revelling in the way her eagerness matched his own, the way her body moved with that drugging, mind-blowingly erotic rhythm beneath his own.

Separating for the few moments it took to remove her T-shirt and then his own was tantalising torment. The pert, aroused breasts gleamed in the starlight, a tempting banquet no red-blooded male could resist.

Deliberately tormenting her while holding himself in check, he ran his fingertips over her tight nipples, watching the way her eyes closed and her lips parted on a sigh of unadulterated pleasure. Bianca, registering his sinfully sexy tone as he asked, 'Does this bore you, *mia cara*?' answered thickly and decisively.

'No!'

All her defences were down, and she knew that lying to the man she loved, trying to hurt him, had been the most shameful thing she'd ever done.

That he would hurt her in the end was a foregone conclusion and something she would have to learn to live with. Loving him would lead to a level of destruction she couldn't bear to think about, but playing safe, pretending indifference was unworthy.

On a sob of blind emotion she reached out for him, running her hands over his shoulders, down to his taut waistline, felt the tight shudder of desire ripple through him and cried thickly, 'Love me, Cesare—make love to me!'

Dawn was almost upon them when they untangled limbs that felt heavy with satiation. Bianca, brushing the thick tangles of her hair away from her face, felt her heart swell with almost painful tenderness.

She loved him so much! She would stay with him for as long as he wanted her and ask nothing in return. Not his ring on her finger, his name, the privileges his vast wealth could buy. Just let her life be part of his for as much or as little of his future as he was willing to give her.

As he sat up, flexing his impressive shoulder muscles, his broad back turned towards her, she said lightly, her love for him brightening her eyes, 'A night under the stars has a lot to recommend itself! But I guess it's time to make a move?'

She reached out to touch him, to underline the feeling of closeness that had always been theirs after making love, and the brightness faded from her eyes as he flinched away, reaching for his discarded clothing and dressing with a fluid efficiency that put a cool area of distance between them.

Shivering in the cool dawn air and catching her breath to swallow the feeble cry of disbelief at the way he seemed to be blocking her out, Bianca scrambled into her own clothes while Cesare waited, his mouth set in a forbidding line, apparently intent on watching the last of the stars fade from the sky.

When she finally got round to stuffing her feet into her flat-heeled sandals he turned and gave her a cool glance. 'Ready? There's a short cut back. Follow me and watch your footing.'

Just that. Nothing more.

Following as he made his way up the far side of the hollow, Bianca felt a lump of icy dread form around her heart, weighing her down. Was he still frigidly angry? Because she'd had the temerity to end their affair, before he'd been ready to call it a day, because of her snippy, confrontational behaviour ever since he'd laid down his terms?

Was this to be her punishment? The payment he demanded for what he was doing for Helene? Using her when he needed sex and ignoring her the rest of the time!

Could he possibly be that cold and unfeeling?

'Cesare—wait!'

They were walking downhill again. She, like a deferential servant, three paces behind. The brittle silence between them stung her, at complete odds with the soothing murmur of the sea, the chatter of a stream, the distant, lonely cry of a gull.

He stopped. Waited. His face like stone, wiped clean of any expression. 'Yes?'

Panting slightly, more from a mixture of dread and burgeoning anger at the way he was treating her than the brisk pace he had set, she planted her hands on her hips and demanded recklessly, determined to get through this barrier he'd erected at any cost, 'What's wrong? I imagine you'd treat a common prostitute with more respect—at least you'd spare a polite word or two during the time it took to put your trousers back on!'

Her self-admittedly crude taunt, hissed out through

her teeth, left him unaffected. His already taut jawline simply clenched a fraction more before he clipped, 'Having never needed the services of one, I wouldn't know,' and strode on. That was all.

Fighting the impulse to scream after him like a fishwife, Bianca followed. Love hurt but she wouldn't run from it again. She would force him to explain his behaviour, and if this was the pattern he had set for their time here together then she would tell him to get lost!

She might love and want him until thoughts of him filled her days and nights to the exclusion of just about everything else, but she wasn't about to let herself be treated like a no-account tramp!

They were approaching the stone house in the opposite direction from the one they'd used yesterday. It meant crossing the stream and he was waiting there, by the single plank that formed a makeshift bridge.

'There's no handrail and the wood gets slippy,' he explained tersely. 'Give me your hand—no, on second thoughts—' Bending, he scooped her up into his arms and strode across the narrow, slippery plank as if he were walking along a well-paved road.

Bianca clung onto his shoulders, fear coiling inside her as the narrow bridge bent and swayed beneath their combined weight. Not because she thought they might fall into the deep pools, onto the lumpy rocks, but because of the way he was holding her. Like a tiresome sack of potatoes that had to be transported. An irritating chore while her whole body ached for him.

As he dropped her to her feet on the threshold of

the door he'd obviously neglected to close the night before when he'd set out to find her she commanded tightly, 'Talk to me, Cesare. You owe me that much.'

She met his veiled eyes. He looked like an austere stranger, hard-edged and ruthless. She put a hand to her throat where a pulse was beating frantically and willed him to say something. Anything.

There had to be an explanation for the way he was acting. Trouble was, she was pretty sure she knew what it was.

'Of course. Later.'

The concession came but it didn't give her any hope for an outcome she could live with. Last night shouldn't have happened, she told herself wretchedly. It had made everything so much worse, binding her stupid heart more closely to him, getting her in deeper than it was safe or sensible to be.

She should have stuck to her original idea of making him back off but it was too late now. She had hated the thought of hurting him, demeaning him, wounding his pride. Love had won but had left her the loser.

Miserably, she watched him walk inside the house, his shoulders as hard and as rigid as the look he turned on her when he said, 'I need to shower first. Make the coffee, would you?'

At any other time during their passionate relationship he would have insisted she join him, not relegated her to the role of skivvy. She was seeing a side of her lover she had never seen before, the side that made him such a formidable business opponent, top dog in his field, earning him the awed respect of staff and rivals alike.

Bianca shuddered convulsively. Their affair, which had been inevitable since they'd first set eyes on each other, had developed into a relationship that had delighted and enthralled her and had eventually imprisoned her within the strands of love. And seeing the danger ahead of her she had struggled to get out. Now it had turned sour, his treatment of her this morning reinforcing everything she had always known.

Cesare Andriotti had no time in his life for commitment, no room in his heart for love. He simply didn't believe in its existence.

Dispiritedly, she began to make coffee.

As Cesare left the bathroom, dressed now in fresh denims and a stark black shirt, the aroma of freshly brewed coffee hit him and his heart clenched.

Last night had been a huge mistake; it had made doing the right thing a thousand times more difficult. When she'd started to make love to him he'd felt an utter heel, hating the thought of her touching him simply because she was keeping to her side of the infamous bargain he'd forced on her.

Yet he'd wanted her so badly he had literally ached all over.

At least, he thought grimly as he fastened the soft leather strap of his wrist-watch, she had proved herself a liar.

He no more bored her than she bored him! A growing indifference to his love-making hadn't been the real reason for her decision to end their affair—no matter how much the little minx had tried to pretend it had been. He stamped down hard on a sudden and searing stab of elation, on the memory of the long night of exquisite passion. All that was over. *Finito.*

His dark eyes hardening, he headed down the stairs. Whatever her real reasons, he told himself firmly, no doubt she thought them sound. And he had no right to demand the continuation of the affair simply because the thought of it ending left him in the unusual and uncomfortable position of feeling bereft.

She was already pouring coffee into two earthenware mugs when he entered the room. He murmured her name, Bianca, inside the privacy of his head. A plea? A yearning for something he couldn't put a name to?

He tightened his mouth. He'd get over it, whatever it was. He'd find a replacement, no trouble. If he could be bothered. Right at this moment he couldn't imagine anyone else in her place.

He'd get over that, too.

'Coffee smells good.' He sketched a smile. Poor little Bee! No wonder she'd lashed out at him with that taunt about prostitutes! But putting distance between them had been necessary. Vital. Still was.

Allowing things to go back to the way they'd always been between them, the feeling of close companionship after great sex, laughter, gentle teasing, would have robbed him of all his will-power. And he needed every last bit of it if he were to stick to his intentions and make belated amends for what he had done.

She flicked him a quick look from beneath her lashes and the muscles around Cesare's heart contracted. She looked exhausted. Bianca Jay, normally so perfectly groomed, cool and sophisticated, had grass stalks in her wildly tumbled hair, her workman-like clothes were grubby and decidedly rumpled, her soft mouth drooping, her huge, usually sparkling eyes looked hurt and bewildered.

The urge to close the distance between them, take her in his arms, tell her she looked adorable, kiss those soft lips until she smiled for him again, take care of her, was almost irresistible.

Denying it with all the will-power at his command, he took one of the mugs she'd placed on the table. Took a long, much-needed swallow, made a production of looking at his watch to buy himself a second or two of time and said tonelessly, 'I have to go if I'm to be back in London later today.' He set the mug back on the table. 'I suggest you move into the villa for a few days to satisfy yourself that Helene is settling in. I'd tell you to stay as long as you like but I know you're anxious to get back to work.'

Another look at his watch, a glance through the small window, anything to stop himself from looking at her, watching the look of painful bewilderment flicker over her expressive features. 'I'll be using the 'copter, of course, but when you're ready to leave Marco will arrange for Giovanni to ferry you to Palermo in the launch. There are daily, non-stop flights to London.'

'What are you saying?' Bianca could barely get the words out. She felt as if she were suffocating. Pulling out a chair from the table, she sat down heavily, convinced that her legs were about to give way beneath her.

She searched his face for any sign of softening. Nothing. His shatteringly handsome features were stark and he looked as if he would never smile again. Or certainly not for her.

As she laved her suddenly dry and tremulous lips he turned his head away and answered harshly, 'That you are free to go. I forced you to come here. It was a despicably dishonourable thing to do. You wanted to end our affair and, at that time, I did not. But that is no excuse for what I did. I give you my apologies, and your wish. It is over.'

Not meeting her eyes, he dipped his raven-dark head in her direction and strode out through the door.

CHAPTER SEVEN

'WHY won't you move in here with us?'

Helene pouted as she filled two cups from the coffee-pot. 'We live in the lap of luxury here and I could see more of you than a ten-minute flying visit each morning. And you'd be company for Jeanne. Besides, don't you get lonely now Cesare's gone?' Her voice sharpened, anxiety etching into her tone. 'Please don't tell me you're hoping he'll change his mind and come back? You're being a fool to yourself if you do. He definitely said his next visit would be when he joined the family holiday at the end of the summer.'

Bianca reluctantly dragged her eyes from the view from the terrace, the sparkling sea that danced to the shore and broke in curling foam against the pebbles, and gave her attention back to her mother.

'Because I don't want to eat into the time you spend with your professor.'

That wasn't the real reason she had refused to move into the villa, of course it wasn't; it was nowhere near it. Since Cesare had left three days ago she'd been feeling too wretched, too confused about her own feelings to be able to keep up a relaxed front for more than ten minutes or so at a time. She wasn't fit company for anyone.

Bianca stirred her coffee and found a smile from

somewhere, adding, 'Besides, I enjoy fending for my-self, just chilling out. And Giovanni brings fresh pro-duce every day. This morning it was quail—I shall have fun figuring out how to cook it!'

'Really?' Helene commented drily. She didn't look in the least impressed by the blithe, 'all's well with my world' act, Bianca noted, and quickly changed the subject.

'How are things going with your professor?'

She was sure he knew what he was doing. Helene looked far more relaxed than she had done for almost as long as Bianca could remember. Instead of con-stantly fiddling with her hair, her jewellery, playing with her teaspoon, her mother's hands were folded in her lap, resting on the soft blue cotton of her sundress.

'Marco. His name is Marco. People pay through the nose to attend his private clinics—did you know that? Anyway, we get along remarkably well. He's a relax-ing person to be around. We walk, we talk and some-times we simply sit and listen to music.'

'Right. Good.'

What else was there to say? Professor Vaccari was obviously playing a softly-softly game. Perhaps he wanted his patient completely relaxed, physically fit-ter, before he made her face up to her past trauma and enabled her to finally put it behind her.

Not knowing a thing about the kind of therapy Helene was undergoing, Bianca decided it made no sense at all to probe deeper, and, casting around for something to say to keep her mother off the subject of Cesare's disappearance because she really didn't want to have to talk about him, she asked in what she hoped passed for a tone of idle curiosity, 'Where's Jeanne this morning?'

'Wandering.' Helene gave an impatient sigh. 'She isn't used to having nothing to do. Marco suggested she occupied herself by making a collection of the wild flowers here on the island—pressing them and so on. So she left after breakfast wearing the most ridiculous sun-hat I've ever seen. I'm actually thinking of asking her if she'd like to leave when you do. As a holiday it simply isn't working for her. She won't sunbathe, she won't swim—she's too old and stout, so she says, for such things—and she keeps worrying about leaving her house unoccupied. I really can't think why she was invited in the first place.'

'Cesare thought she'd keep you company while you settled in,' Bianca said.

She only realised she'd walked right into a trap and steered the conversation where she hadn't wanted it to go when Helene leaned back in her chair, narrowed her eyes and remarked drily, 'And you, darling? You were obviously meant to keep him company, or why would he have whisked you away to some stone shack or other? And why, after a mere twenty-four hours, did he take himself off? Is he giving you the runaround?'

Suspicion of men's motives had marred her mother's life for as long as Bianca could remember. Helene craved male adulation because it shored up her self-confidence, which had been decidedly shaky since Bianca's father had traded her in for a newer model.

But she had never trusted any of her lovers enough to give her heart. It was still too preoccupied with her twisted love-hate feelings for her former husband.

Bianca swallowed jerkily. Now was the time to tell her mother what she wanted to hear, to make what had happened real and final.

She lifted her cup and drained the contents, buying time. Her reluctance to admit their affair was over made no kind of sense. To protect herself from further emotional damage she'd wanted her relationship with Cesare to end, hadn't she? So why was she so superstitiously afraid of putting it into words?

'You were right,' she said as coolly as she was able. 'Cesare and I were involved.' The hand that replaced her cup on its saucer shook. Bianca prayed her mother hadn't noticed. 'But not any more. It's over.'

The spoken admission made her shiver, her stomach clenching in a tight, cold knot. And in the few beats of assimilating silence she concentrated hard on the whisper of the sea, the cry of a bird, the heat of the sun on her bare arms and on the length of her legs exposed by her neat white shorts.

Concentrated on anything to stop herself from weeping and reinforcing Helene's fears that history was about to repeat itself.

'And you're happy about that?' Helene probed quietly, leaning forward.

Forced to meet her mother's eyes, Bianca knew she wouldn't be able to manage a smile and made up for it by giving a slight shrug, fishing her sunglasses from the back pocket of her shorts and putting them on. 'It was never serious.'

That had been the understanding, the point made by both of them at the outset. Things had turned out very differently for her.

The smile of sheer relief on Helene's face lifted it from the gauntness of the past few months to a semblance of her once vibrant loveliness. 'That's all right, then—if you're sure? Darling—' she reached out a hand, sunlight glittering on her rings, and Bianca took it, her bones smarting from the pressure '—I'm truly, truly grateful to your former boyfriend, please don't think I'm not. He's been more than generous. But I'd have warned you off him long ago if I'd known you were involved, that he was the man you'd been with when you crept home at dawn. He's what? Thirty-fourish? And unmarried, rich as sin and handsome as the devil. That puts him firmly in Category B.'

A bubble of near hysterical amusement at the idea of anyone trying to squash the proud and self-confident Italian into any kind of category produced the first smile Bianca had given since Cesare had left her. 'Category B?' she queried on a squeak.

'Men who would rather die than be married,' Helene answered acidly. 'They have the looks and the money to attract whomsoever they fancy at the moment, then they ditch them when the novelty wears off. If they marry at all it will be some time in their late sixties when their looks and energy are going. Then they'll use their wealth to buy some gorgeous young thing to boost their egos and dance attendance on them in their declining years.'

'Cynical!' Bianca chided, removing her hand from her mother's grasp, surreptitiously massaging her crushed fingers beneath the top of the table as she tried to ignore the much more painful lump in her throat. Helene's character assassination had been spot on.

'And Category A?' she asked as a diversion.

'The man I married. Your father. The restless serial husband forever in search of the next younger, prettier trophy wife.'

Alarm bells rang as Bianca noted the familiar bitter tone. She said gently, 'It was a long time ago. You must try to put it behind you. Brooding about it only makes you unhappy.' And turn to the bottle, she added inside her head and wondered how her mother was managing in this alcohol-free zone but didn't dare to ask.

Helene's mouth tightened. 'Easy enough to say if you don't know what you're talking about! If you ever fall in love, and I mean really in love, you'll realise that forgetting isn't that easy. And when you do fall for someone make sure he's not a love rat. Find a nice, ordinary guy who'll still love you when you get wrinkles and begin to sag all over!'

The arrival of Professor Vaccari, followed by Maria with a tray of fresh coffee, gave Bianca just the excuse she needed to leap to her feet. She knew now how difficult forgetting could be!

'My dear, please don't let me drive you away!' His open smile encompassed both women as he took one of the vacant chairs at the table, but Bianca backed off, tempering her abrupt departure with, 'I'm going to find a quiet beach for a swim—I might as well make use of what the island has to offer while I'm here.'

'Yes, of course. Talking of which—' Marco Vaccari smiled his thanks at the departing Maria '—Cesare asked me to take care of your travel arrangements when you do decide to leave. It would be helpful if you gave me twenty-four hours' notice.'

'And don't make it too soon, darling,' Helene put in, pouring for the professor. 'The agency won't fall to pieces if you're away for a couple of weeks. And join us for dinner tonight—promise? I don't see nearly enough of you.'

'I'm cooking quail, remember?' Bianca passed that off with ease. After half an hour, at most, her efforts to appear relaxed, without a care in her head, would be wearing thin. 'Tomorrow, maybe.'

By tomorrow she might have got her confused emotions back into some kind of order, be able to hear Cesare's name without feeling the familiar tug of misery, the sting of tears behind her eyes, the draining sense of loss, she told herself without a great deal of hope as she skirted the imposing villa and headed inland.

At least the information that she and Cesare were history had laid her mother's fears at rest. She didn't want to give her anything to worry about while the long haul of her recovery was in its initial phase.

She would always be grateful to Cesare for giving Helene this opportunity, even if the price he'd initially demanded had been cruelly high. And perhaps the hardest part of all was the way he'd relented, realised how wrong he'd been and apologised.

It showed he did have principles and only served to make her love him more.

And loving him at all was the very last thing she wanted.

Standing under the shower as the long hot afternoon drew to a close, Bianca closed her eyes as the water sluiced away the salt and sand from her tired body.

She had explored every inch of the island, swum from the most secluded cove she could find and gazed out to sea, wondering how such a perfect place could seem like purgatory. But not for much longer; she'd be leaving at the end of the week. Tomorrow she'd ask Marco to make the travel arrangements for both herself and Jeanne.

Having come across her aunt as the older woman had been trudging back to the villa around noon, she had noted the disgruntled look on the red, perspiring face beneath the battered-into-strange-shapes sun-hat, the unsuitable flowered nylon dress, the swollen ankles and heavy walking shoes. 'You look in need of a long cold drink. How's it going?' she asked with sympathy.

'Don't ask!' Jeanne waved a bunch of wilting flowers under Bianca's nose. 'I've been packed off to make a collection of wild flowers—like a Victorian child! I was looking forward to this holiday—I didn't realise there'd be nothing to do. No shops, no little cafés where I could sit and people watch. Helene spends most of her time with the professor, understandably, so she doesn't need my company and you're behaving like a hermit! It wouldn't be so bad if I could make myself useful around the villa. But Maria won't hear of it. There's an army of servants for just the three of us.' She huffed out a disapproving breath. 'None of them speaks more than two words of English—apart from Maria, who apparently doesn't think it's quite the thing to chat with the guests, and Ugo who flew your Signor Andriotti away in the helicopter. And he, Ugo, is only interested in flirting with the maids. He's some kind of steward, from what I could gather. He'll probably be back any time now, flashing his white teeth and posturing for all those giggly girls! Strutting his stuff, I think you young ones call it!'

Bianca smothered a smile. Jeanne was plainly bored out of her socks and greatly disapproving of the absent Ugo. Making up her mind there and then, she said, 'I'll be leaving for London at the end of the week. Would you like to come with me?'

She should have spent more time with her aunt, she recognised guiltily, not hidden away, licking her wounds. It was time she got on with her life and stopped mourning over a lost lover. She would not let herself follow in Helene's self-destructive footsteps!

Now, drying herself on one of the huge fleecy towels, she decided to walk over to the villa right now and ask Marco to make those travel arrangements, for the two of them.

Helene wouldn't be pleased; she had obviously wanted her to stay on for another week at least. But she had her own life to lead, the shattered pieces to pick up, and over the years her mother had become far too dependent on her for emotional support and the day-to-day practicalities of their lives.

It would be a wrench, Bianca knew that, but if Helene was to make progress she would have to learn to stand on her own feet, take responsibility for her own life. It would not be easy for either of them, she conceded sadly. Looking out for her mother had become the major part of her life.

In the bedroom she and Cesare were to have shared, and hadn't, she selected a cool, sleeveless silky shift in shades of cream and amber and a pair of low-heeled strappy sandals. Leaving her dark hair loose to her shoulders, her only make-up a little moisturiser, she decided she'd pass muster for an early evening visit.

She wouldn't stay long, just relay her request and wander back and decide whether she could be bothered cooking the quail.

Leaving the little stone house, she heard the unmistakable sound of the helicopter blades and her heart jumped into her mouth. Then settled back into its normal position, although still feeling decidedly fluttery.

It would be the posturing Ugo, of course it would, back from the fleshpots of Sicily, probably bringing in fresh supplies.

How could she, even for one moment, have clutched at the hope it might be Cesare? He had made it crystal clear that they wouldn't be seeing each other again.

Taking a few minutes to recapture her errant breath, she chided herself for that moment of terrifyingly soar-

ing hope. She had wanted a clean break and finally
he'd given it to her, so how could she be stupid
enough to want to see him one more time? Her battered heart was already hurting badly enough, so why
twist a knife in it?

On that eminently sensible thought, she gathered
herself together and began to walk along the track,
taking her time because she didn't want to confront
her mother in a state of breathless agitation. That lady
had very finely tuned antennae where her daughter was
concerned.

In the event there was no sign of her. Bianca
mounted the steps to the terrace where the evening
meal was to be taken. The table was set for three, fine
linen, costly silver, candles already flaming steadily
within glass holders.

And the dashing young man, resplendent in tightly
sheathing cream-coloured jodhpurs and a flowing
black shirt, just had to be Ugo. He seemed to be over-
seeing a dimpling doe-eyed maid who was placing a
crystal jug of iced water on the table, the only liquid
refreshment that would be served with the meal.

'The elusive signorina!' Ugo padded forward as
soon as he became aware of her presence. Bianca
noted the predatory gleam in his black eyes as he
swaggered towards her. In a studiedly languid movement he lifted her hand, kissed the backs of her fingers
and said in heavily accented English, 'How may I help
you? Are you to dine with your family? I do hope so,
one so beautiful should not hide herself away.'

Suppressing a snort of wry laughter, Bianca explained, 'I'm not staying. I just want a few words with the professor.'

No wonder her strait-laced aunt disapproved of him, she thought as he dismissed the obviously piqued maid with a shooing movement of his free hand. Far too handsome, far too obvious and far too fond of himself, as far as Bianca was concerned he was a joke. She wondered how often he practised that slightly lop-sided, would-be seductive smile in front of the mirror and decided that, although his teeth might be very white, they were too big.

She tugged at her hand, trying to remove it from his grasp, but his fingers merely tightened as he husked, 'If you were mine I also would hide you away, but I would not leave you!'

This was going beyond a joke! She opened her mouth to tell him as much; it stayed that way, but no words came. Her throat had tightened with shock.

Cesare, closely followed by the professor, had emerged onto the terrace from open French windows. In a casual, cream-coloured suit, his dark shirt open at the neck, he looked fantastic. Heat rushed through her body and the shock of seeing him again, when she'd thought she never would, stopped her breathing.

Tension had hardened his bronzed features and his narrowed eyes looked black with temper as he vented a string of harsh Italian that had Ugo stiffening, dropping her hand as if it were a red-hot coal and muttering something in the same language that sounded decid-edly defensive before sloping away towards the rear of the villa.

He must have flown in with Ugo, she decided, and whatever had brought him back it certainly wasn't the pleasure of her company. Dull colour stained his high cheekbones and his mouth looked so furious she shuddered with reaction.

Then pulled herself together. His reasons for being here were no business of hers. This was his island, his villa; she was the interloper.

Dragging her eyes from the now savage glitter of his, she fastened them on the professor who was trying to disguise a wicked grin, cleared her clogged throat and stated, 'My aunt and I would like to leave—'

She got no further because Marco Vaccari let the grin rip, casting a sidelong glance at his glowering compatriot as he inserted, 'Jeanne has already told me of your intentions and the matter is in hand. Unfortunately the earliest commercial flight I could book you on is Monday next. I hope that won't inconvenience you?'

Hell! Another five days on the island instead of the two she'd been counting on. Impatience to get back to some kind of normality made her grit her teeth. At least the company jet hadn't been called into service; she didn't want to owe Cesare any more than she already did. And she managed, more or less, gracefully, 'No, of course not. You'll want my credit-card details.'

'It has been taken care of.'

Sheer frustration balled her hands into fists. Whichever way she turned she got deeper in debt to her former lover. She loathed the feeling of being a paid-off mistress! Refusing to look at Cesare, who was burning holes in her skin with the intensity of a gaze she could feel and didn't want to have to see, she watched as the professor wandered down to the table and wondered why he seemed to find the whole situation vastly amusing.

'You will join us for dinner?' His eyes twinkled at her. 'Your mother and aunt will be down at any moment. We would all be so pleased to have your company.'

'Sorry.' Bianca sketched a thin smile. 'I have a date with a quail.' And turned to head back the way she had come, forcing herself not to run.

She was behaving childishly, she scolded herself. Not giving Cesare as much as a 'hello' was not only juvenile, but ill-mannered. She should have been able to handle the situation with more sophistication; he would expect that from his ex-lovers.

She was still breathing shakily after that unexpected encounter. He'd as good as said they wouldn't be seeing each other again, so finding him here had been a shock to her system, especially since she'd done nothing but think of him over the last three days.

An arm casually draped around her shoulder had her feet stumbling to a standstill, her heart jumping to her throat and suffocating her. 'Wait for me,' Cesare said, then urged her forward with the gentle pressure of his hand. 'And a word of warning, give young Ugo a wide berth. He's a dyed-in-the-wool womaniser.'

'It takes one to know one!' The tart words were out before she could stop them. Bianca's feet slewed to a

stop again, her skin flushing with shame. 'I'm sorry,
that was uncalled for.'

Insults would get her nowhere and would only serve
to demean what they had once had. Shrugging his arm
away, she stole a look at him beneath the heavy fringes
of her lashes and looked swiftly away.

He was smiling, damn him! Smiling with that quick
brilliance that took her breath away. His being here,
being close, wasn't helping her recovery one iota. It
was putting it into reverse. But he wasn't being deliberately cruel. He didn't know how deeply she loved
him. Had never known. Would never know.

Walking on, she questioned unsteadily, 'What
brings you back?' She knew it wasn't simply to torment her. As far as he was concerned she was the one
who had wanted to end their affair and he had eventually agreed. He would have put her very firmly behind him so it seemed the right question to ask. Polite
conversation.

'I left something behind.'

Had his accent thickened, his voice grown huskier?
Something quite terrifying inched down Bianca's
spine. Stop it! she told herself, quickening her pace.
Stop looking for something that isn't there!

'Right,' she responded gruffly, though what he'd
left behind she couldn't imagine—nothing that she'd
seen lying around, that was for sure.

'And I have something of importance I need to discuss with you.'

They had reached the little house and Bianca had
her hand on the grainy, sun-warmed planks of the

door. With sudden insight she said, 'I'm glad. I wanted to talk to you, too. About the lease on the Hampstead house. I don't want you to do anything about it. Our—' again she felt her face flush fiercely '—our bargain no longer stands. You're already doing a great deal for Helene and I'll always be truly grateful for that, but that must be as far as it goes.'

'Ah,' he said softly, so softly she felt the impact of that single syllable feather lightly over every inch of her skin, and the way he was looking at her, as if he had a secret that pleased him, made her very nervous.

How he had missed her! Cesare's veiled eyes travelled from the shining fall of her hair to those beautiful, anxious eyes, the lush curve of her mouth and the body beneath the soft silk she was wearing.

All mine! he thought possessively, stamping down the imperative, hungry need to close the small distance between them, to hold that tempting body against his, devour her mouth, lose himself in her answering passion.

He had to wait. Rushing things wouldn't get him what he wanted.

Opening the door for her, he ushered her into the darkening room and told her gently, 'The lease has already been taken care of. The Hampstead house is Helene's for as long as she wants it.'

'No!' Bianca gasped, her eyes challenging his in the dying light. Frustration was burning a hole in her brain, her eyes glittering with sudden angry tears. 'You can't do that!'

'It is already done. The documents were signed this morning.'

Bianca closed her eyes to block him out and clamped her mouth shut to stop herself from screaming in frustration. And when she'd won control back she gritted, 'Then somehow I'll pay back every penny. I may have been your mistress but I won't be paid off! The thought of it makes my skin crawl—so if this is what you came to discuss you may as well take yourself off right now! I've said all I'm going to on the subject. I'll repay every penny if it takes me the rest of my life!'

'*Cara*,' he soothed, moving just a little closer, his eyes softening. 'What I have done has nothing to do with anything as crude as a pay-off for services rendered. You mustn't even think that. I want to help. I—' He bit off the rest of the sentence before the impetuous words were out.

She wouldn't want the burden of his confession of love. Bianca Jay wasn't into that kind of emotional commitment. Her mother's experiences and the resultant mess she'd made of her life were responsible for that. Forcing a smile, a light tone, he added, 'Discussing the lease was not on my agenda.'

'Then what is?' she threw at him, stung beyond bearing by what she translated as the thread of amusement in his voice.

Wishing the question unasked when he turned to flick on the light and sauntered slowly in the direction of the stairs, telling her, 'That is for me to know, but you'll find out later. After I've showered. I think you mentioned quail. I'm looking forward to it. Be a good girl and open the wine, hmm?'

Slowly, slowly, he told himself as he mounted the stairs. His instinct to turn back, to take her in his arms, run his hands over her lovely body, kiss her until she responded with the sheer magic of that passion he had begun to crave above all else was completely out of order.

If he were to get her to agree to what he wanted more than anything else in this world, then his arguments must be slanted to appeal to the rational part of her mind.

And he could do it! he thought on a sharp stab of triumph. When it came to the negotiating table, no one could best him!

CHAPTER EIGHT

SEETHING now, her emotions in utter turmoil, Bianca watched Cesare turn the corner at the head of the stairs and disappear.

Open the wine, like a good girl—yes, sir! Anything you say, sir! she fulminated spikily.

Dish up the quail—oh, yeah?

Savagely disgruntled, Bianca reached the plate with the two small birds Giovanni had presented her with this morning out of the fridge and thumped it down on the table. If Cesare wanted quail for supper he could darn well cook for himself. She had lost her appetite.

Stamping over to the open door, she crossed her arms over her chest and leaned against the frame, breathing in great and hopefully calming gulps of the soft evening air. She could smell the sea and the sweetly sharp aromatic scent of wild rosemary.

According to the principles of aromatherapy, wasn't rosemary supposed to clear the head and clarify thoughts? Well, in her case, it wasn't working!

For the life of her she couldn't figure out what he was doing here.

Using the place as a comfort station after his flight from London?

No, of course not, that didn't make any sense at all. Facilities back at the villa were far superior—great sunken marble baths, large enough to accommodate an entire football team, five-course gourmet meals, an army of willing servants to tend to his every need.

And he hadn't come to collect something he'd left behind because there wasn't anything, unless he meant the clothes in the hanging cupboard. Which didn't make the remotest sense, either.

Just knock-around casual gear, which he surely wouldn't have been pining for. He had an apartment in London, another in New York, a villa—quite superb by all accounts—in the hills above Rome. Each would house a wardrobe of exclusive designer statements suitable for every possible occasion.

Which left the lease.

Bianca gritted her teeth until her jaw ached. The thought of the amount of money he must have spent on that sent her blood pressure into the stratosphere. But he'd said that news of the extended lease hadn't been on his agenda. In any case it could easily have waited until she was back in London, the contentious matter dealt with through their solicitors.

Attempting to work out his motives for being here would probably give her permanent brain damage, but at least it took her mind off the other aspect. The pleasure/pain of seeing him again, being close to him physically if not emotionally, the quiver of sensual excitement that made her will-power crumple when she looked at him, the loving him, always loving him, that now seemed to be her unenviable destiny.

'Insubordination suits you.'

She hadn't heard him come to stand behind her. His voice, honeyed, smooth and slow was like a lingering caress. It made her breath catch in her throat, her pulse rate go haywire and sent feathery flutters of sensation down the length of her spine.

'I wouldn't jump to fill your orders either!' he offered lightly. But he would, he knew he would. He'd jump through hoops and back again if she asked him to!

He put his hands on her shoulders, just lightly, very lightly, nothing sexual, nothing to kindle the conflagration that ignited wildly when they touched each other. Easy did it. Nice and easy...

He could feel the tension in the slender bones beneath his fingertips. Feel the transmission of heat. Gently, he turned her to face him and immediately dropped his hands to his sides in case the temptation to go on touching, to massage those tight muscles until they relaxed for him, until she looped her arms around his neck and drew his head down for a kiss that would send them both into orbit, overrode his common sense.

Sex for them had always been out of this world. But it wasn't the way forward. If it had been he wouldn't have been facing a certain battle of wills. Rational persuasion was the only way forward.

Forcing his gaze from the long amber eyes that always, since the first time of seeing her, had made him feel as if he were drowning, he said softly, 'Let's face the cooking together, shall we? It will be a first and I'm always open to new experiences.'

Like the intriguing possibilities of a new mistress when the current one began to pall, she thought dourly, then squashed the uncharitable thought because he was only talking of cooking together.

He had cooked for her on their first evening here; previously they'd eaten out or the estimable, multi-talented Denton had rustled up something tempting at Cesare's London apartment. Steeling herself, she followed him back into the large living-room-cum-kitchen.

He had changed into a vest-style T-shirt that drew her eyes to those broad shoulders and strong arms, the tanned skin that gleamed like polished silk. And the stone-coloured jeans that clipped his neat backside and moulded his long thighs were positively sinful.

Ignoring the all-too-customary lurch of her heart, the hot, pulsating sensation that flooded her system, she joined him at the table. If he wanted to play house then she would be wise to humour him. Asking him why he was here when everything was well and truly over between them, when his presence gave her equal measures of delight and anguish, making everything impossible for her, would be far too dangerous.

'What do we do with these?' She pointed at the quail, her tone matching his for lightness, or at least she hoped it did. 'Roast them like chickens, or what?'

'Whenever I've been served quail it comes wrapped

in bacon.' He gave her a soft, sideways smile. 'Do we have any?'

'I'll see.' She'd meant to sound cool and not too interested, but she'd just sounded breathless. Why had what he'd just said made it sound as if they were a couple when they both knew they weren't?

Rooting in the fridge gave her the excuse she needed to move well away from him, cool down her fevered brain. And when she finally emerged with the bacon she could have put her hands on immediately, had she been so minded, he had finished setting the oven at some probably guessed-at temperature and was crashing around in a wall cupboard for a roasting pan, she noted, resentment for what he was doing to her— and for that dratted lease—making her eyes mutinous and her mouth tighten and turn down at the corners.

'There were herbs, as I remember, made into a stuffing. Choose some, would you, while I act the gentleman and chop an onion?' A pause, a simmering look in his dark smoky eyes that made the space between them sizzle until she felt hot and frenzied, then, 'Friends now, Bee?'

He gave her that totally disarming grin of his and she melted. If she could separate friend from lover, compartmentalise the two aspects of their relationship that had previously gone hand in hand, it would be infinitely preferable to getting so wound up that she ended up, as she surely would, instigating an emotional shouting match. Surely she could manage that for a couple of hours, the time it would take to cook supper and eat it?

So friends, for the space of time it took to make a meal, was what she would aim for. And after he'd eaten he would surely go, leave her to nurse the new wounds he'd inflicted in privacy.

After making that decision, sticking to it, it was easy, well, relatively so, as they worked together, creating an enormous salad—having quirky arguments over what to put in it, and compromising by using everything—while the quail sizzled in the oven.

The wine was opened, left to breathe, and Cesare unearthed a folding table and two chairs from an outhouse and carried them down to the side of the stream, placing an ornate oil lamp on the table because it was getting quite dark now.

Inviting her to sit, sharing a corner of cheese with her because both their stomachs were grumbling, his with hunger and hers, she suspected, with the nervous tension she was doing her best to hide, Cesare poured wine while they waited out the final ten minutes of cooking time. 'I've never done this before. Dined with my feet in ferns, on food cooked by two bumbling, amicable amateurs, at a table that looks as though it might fall to pieces at any moment.' He raised his glass to hers. 'To the simple life.'

'I'll drink to that!'

But her reply to the toast had a hollow ring and she hoped he hadn't picked up on it. If he saw them now as just good friends, then she owed it to herself to go along with it. But there was nothing simple about the way she was feeling.

After the way they had parted she had no idea why he'd returned, why his mood was so different. He complicated everything! Seeing him again deepened her sense of loss, of desperate desolation.

The game birds were not only edible but actually perfectly cooked. They congratulated each other, and Bianca managed most of her share before her throat finally closed up with nerves.

If she asked him why he was here he probably wouldn't give her a straight answer, any more than he had done earlier. And was he intending to stay the night, or was he going back to the villa?

The latter, she devoutly hoped. He had agreed that their affair was over. So why would he want to sleep in the other twin-bedded room when he had all the luxury and convenience of the other place at his disposal?

And surely to goodness he wasn't expecting to sleep with her! It was over. He'd agreed! He couldn't expect one last night together for old times' sake, could he? And if he did would she be strong enough to resist?

The prickles of excitement deep inside her at the mere thought of what might happen told her that her ability to resist him was zero, and that would be catastrophic because it would put any progress she had made towards erasing her love for him into sharp reverse!

She was getting so wound up she could barely sit

still, never mind watch his relaxed mood, and when the insects began to bite she had the perfect excuse.

'I think I'll turn in, something's decided to snack on my legs.'

The catch in her voice betrayed her inner tension but his lazy, 'I guess you're absolutely right,' told her that, thankfully, he hadn't picked up on it.

He got to his feet exactly when she did. In the pool of lamplight he looked strangely mysterious, nerve-quiveringly dangerous, the planes and angles of his face thrown into harsh relief. A convulsive shudder, delicious and scary, rushed through her tense body. He was so gorgeous, he was everything she wanted. Everything she couldn't have.

To disguise an anguished whimper, Bianca bent to scratch an itchy lump on her ankle and wished he'd do the right thing and say goodnight, walk away. In a minute she would make a fool of herself and burst into tears!

'Don't scratch!' Cesare chided gently. 'There's a tube of ointment in the kitchen cabinet where the sticking plasters and aspirins are kept. Use it after you've showered.'

Swallowing around the lump in her throat, she said a muffled, 'Thanks' and scrambled up towards the house. A few paces on, she stopped. Turned. He had every right to expect more than a headlong flight. Friends, he'd said. So friendliness was what he'd get; any deviation from that path would let him know that her emotions ran much deeper than that.

He wouldn't be able to see her clearly in the darkness and that was a bonus, and he'd moved out of the pool of lamplight so she couldn't see him properly, either, and that was another bonus.

Finding a note of something approaching cheerfulness, she said, 'Thanks for your help. Making supper was fun. You'll need the torch to find your way back—you know where it is, help yourself. 'Night, Cesare.'

A slow pulse of silence, then, 'Goodnight, Bee.' And that was it, all there was. Making herself walk at a normal pace, Bianca made it into the house, then flew up the stairs. She didn't want to be around when he followed to collect the torch. She didn't want to have to see him again. Ever. It hurt too much.

Standing under the warm, soothing water of the shower, Bianca reflected miserably that she knew now exactly why he had spent the evening with her, what he had intended to discuss.

Despite that earlier uncharacteristic descent into blackmail—for which, she reminded herself fairly, he had apologised—Cesare Andriotti was a civilised man. He was faithful and loyal while his affairs lasted and was too urbane and sophisticated to want to see them end acrimoniously.

So in the end there had been no need to have that discussion. 'Friends, Bee?' he'd asked and to protect herself she'd gone right along with it.

Since she'd been the one to end their affair in the first place, he could have no idea of her true feelings for him. He couldn't begin to imagine how being forced into his company, compelled to play-act, had been sheer, unmitigated torment.

A flood of tears mingled with the needle spray of the shower. Goodbye, Cesare, she said inside her head. And started to sob.

Cesare fetched the torch and went back to extinguish the oil lamp, taking his time over clearing everything away.

There had been a few spiky moments—such as when she'd blown a gasket over that lease—but on the whole the evening had gone to plan.

Plan One to kick off with. Nice and easy on the surface. She could have no idea how he'd ached to take her in his arms, make love to her, explain the self-knowledge that had hit him like a thunderbolt when he'd got back to London, how the ache had turned into a physical pain.

Opening the door of the small medicine cupboard, he extracted the tube of ointment, switched off the kitchen light and mounted the stairs.

Time to put Plan Two into operation. Letting her know he would still be here in the morning.

There was a strip of light showing beneath the door of the bedroom she was using, the room they were to have shared until he'd come to his senses and realised just how deplorable his behaviour was.

The air in his lungs felt thick and heavy as he tapped on the door, probably inaudibly, and pushed it open. And just stood there, on the threshold, his heart-beats ratcheting up a gear as he fought to hold onto his determination not to make any sexual advances in any way, shape or form.

She was sitting on the edge of one of the beds, naked. A muscle jerked convulsively in his throat. His heart skipped a beat. Her body was perfection and he knew it so well, every tempting, warm and willing inch of it. The high, firm, beautiful breasts, the curve of her slender arms, the indentation of her tiny waist, the soft mound of curls at the apex of her thighs, the utter magic of her...

If he touched her, and one touch was all it had ever needed, she would share the magic of her body with him tonight. He knew that. They had never been able to resist each other.

But this wasn't about sex. This was about something on a different level.

Her eyes had darkened as he'd made that regrettably smouldering appraisal and then she made a dive for the towel, formerly discarded on the floor, and held it in front of her in an act of belated and, in their case, unnecessary modesty.

It was the act of his life, but he managed a small smile, a contrite, 'I'm sorry. I didn't mean to startle you.' He aimed the tube of ointment in her direction and watched it fall with a gentle plop on the sprigged cotton coverlet at her side. Then, forcing his hungry gaze away from the unendurable temptation of her, he strode over the narrow, polished boards and whisked the pillow and crisp cotton sheets from the other, un-occupied bed.

'What are you doing?'

'Making a bed up in the other room,' he answered her strangled question, heading back to the door before the temptation to stay, to run his hands through the heavy, silky fall of her hair, down the cleanly graceful line of her spine, to fasten his hands on her hips, lift her, turn her and draw her towards the throbbing, eager evidence of his manhood, got the better of him.

'See you in the morning,' he managed before he closed the door to her bedroom behind him, then stumbled into the other room and let out a long, shuddering sigh.

Plan Two successfully started. Though right at this moment the consolation was pretty thin.

Dropping his gleanings from her room onto the nearest bed, he walked over to the window and stared out at the starry night. Abstinence from the exquisite pleasure they'd always been able to give each other would be a small price to pay if the end result meant he got what he wanted.

Bianca Jay as his wife.

And he always got what he wanted, didn't he?

He had five days to prove to her—as a starting point—that they could find pleasure in each other's company without sex. Prove that they could be buddies, best friends. That they could live together harmoniously, with mutual respect and consideration.

Five days.

As soon as he'd known that he had to have her permanently in his life, that the initial offer of marriage that had so shocked him at the time had been his instincts telling him what his mind was too closed to admit, he'd phoned Marco and told him to forget his former instruction that the company jet would be waiting for Bianca at the Palermo airport when she said she was ready to return to London. His old friend was to book her on a commercial flight—and not put her on standby—which would mean, especially at this time of year, that he had a few days' grace.

Bianca wouldn't trust a declaration of his undying love. It would be the last thing she would want to hear. From her earliest childhood she'd been conditioned to distrust men like himself, men with enough money to buy whatever and whomever they wanted.

He had to teach her to trust him in everything beyond the bedroom door, and when that was accomplished they could go back to being lovers as well as best friends and spend the rest of their lives together as man and wife.

She need never know that without him realising it he'd been falling in love with her throughout their affair.

He had to keep that to himself, though hopefully not throughout their lifetime together. At some stage during the years to come, her trust in him firmly established, she would learn to love. It was all he could hope for, all he wanted.

One last look at the stars and he turned to make up

his single bed. All he had to do was to convince her that they could have a good life together. Close friendship, fun and laughter, great sex.

It would be enough for her to start with, a good beginning, wouldn't it?

CHAPTER NINE

BIANCA crawled out of bed at just before seven the following morning, unable to lie there, sleepless, trying to control the platoon of super-lively butterflies that had taken up residence in her stomach for one more moment.

She felt like death and, peering blearily into the small wall mirror, she knew she looked like it, too.

Eyes puffy from repeated bouts of weeping, supported by bags big enough to pack a picnic in, a mouth that looked sulky and drooping—

Furious with herself for letting Cesare get her in this state, she collected a pair of lemon-yellow shorts and a sleeveless, light cotton, button-through toning shirt and padded to the bathroom.

The warm steam that clouded the mirror and chrome fitments was testimony to the fact that he had risen before her. The tantalising echo of the distinctive aftershave he always used made her heart clench and her eyes glitter with a sudden resurgence of despised tears.

Get a grip, she told herself fiercely as she whipped her short cotton nightshirt over her head. Just grow up, will you? What was there to moan about? By falling in love with him she, and she alone, had brought this emotional mess down on her own head.

Theirs had been a truly adult affair. He'd told her from the outset that he wasn't the marrying kind, obviously to nip any expectations she might have had in that direction neatly and decisively in the bud.

And even if he had been the marrying kind and she'd taken him up on the breathtaking and ill-considered proposal he'd flung at her when she'd told him their affair was over, she wouldn't have been able to trust him not to treat her the way her father had treated her mother, she reminded herself as she brushed her teeth ferociously.

She'd get over him, given time. And the process was starting right this minute!

Half an hour later she descended the stairs, marginally refreshed, her shoulders high and her backbone nicely stiffened, her glossy black hair primly secured back off her face with a trailing, lemon-yellow chiffon scarf.

No sign of Cesare. Bianca didn't know whether to be bitterly disappointed or deeply relieved. The latter, she told herself vehemently. Seeing him, being with him, did her no good at all. With any luck he had gone over to the villa for breakfast, to discuss Helene's progress with the professor.

Her movements deliberately precise, she began to make coffee. The outside door was wide open and it was going to be another glorious day, wall-to-wall sunshine, enough breeze to temper the heat and make the sea dance and glitter.

'Coffee smells good. Just what I needed.'

That all-too-familiar sexy voice stunned her. In the act of reaching for an earthenware mug from the top shelf of the dresser, she froze, the fine hairs on the back of her neck standing to attention, the platoon of butterflies awaking from their brief slumber to dance around with renewed and manic vigour.

She felt as if she were performing in slow motion as the fingers of her right hand closed around the cool surface of one mug, transferred it to her left hand and reached mechanically for another.

Turning slowly, she carefully placed the mugs on a work surface before they dropped from her suddenly nerveless fingers and shattered on the stone floor.

'I thought you'd gone to the villa for breakfast.' Even her voice seemed strange and echoey, as if she were having to push the words through great empty caverns of time and space. Her mangled heart contracted, then started to pound in her eardrums, making her feel dizzy.

He was gorgeous, there was no other word for it. And she loved him, she just couldn't help it, couldn't make it go away.

'No. I was up early and went walking,' he supplied with apparent offhandedness. To take himself out of temptation's way, he thought grittily, to get his priorities straightened out again.

He'd fought a battle royal with himself in the early

hours of the morning, desperately wanting to go to her. Just to lie at her side to watch her wake in the morning, because she'd always refused him that simple yet now all-important pleasure.

He'd wanted to kiss her sleepy eyelids, brush her tousled hair off her face, rub his fingertips over the dreamy, just awakening, curving lips, kiss her there, there and everywhere, hold her warm and boneless body close to his heart, make slow, sensuous love to her…

When the sensible part of his brain, the part that told him to hold his horses, stick to his original agenda, had looked like facing a crashing defeat, he'd hurled himself out of bed, showered in stinging cold water, dressed and taken himself off, walking like a man possessed until he regained his control.

Then back for another shower, hot water to sluice away the sweat and strain, a decent shave, then outside to wait. Wait for her.

And she was worth waiting for. Dressed in cool, fresh yellow, her long legs just lightly tanned, inviting his touch, her breasts tantalisingly free, the lovely curves just discernible beneath the light fabric of her top if he looked hard enough…

The sharp thrust of desire to release that row of pearly buttons from their moorings, part the filmy fabric and run his hands over the shape of her, kiss, suckle, adore was almost too fierce to resist.

Pulling in a jagged breath, he smothered a raw internal groan, poured coffee for them both, pushed the debilitating lustful thoughts right out of his head and asked prosaically, 'Sleep well?'

'Fairly,' she answered with massive overstatement, her skin dampening when he lifted his eyes from his task to connect with hers.

As always, the effect was shattering. Heat curled deep inside her tummy and quivers spread all over her. Sucking breath into her lungs, she noted that this dark, arching brows were pulled together in a tiny frown as he stated the obvious. 'You are very pale.'

Bianca shrugged that aside and lifted her mug, cradling it in both hands. A sleepless, tormented night didn't help a girl greet the morning with glowing radiance! But she could hardly tell him that. He was still watching her closely as he imparted, 'I'll make toast. Would you like an egg to go with it?'

'Nothing for me, but you go ahead.'

Again that slight and puzzling frown. He started to say something, then obviously changed his mind and Bianca left him to it, taking her coffee outside to sit on the bench in the shade.

Cesare had taken away the folding table and chairs he'd unearthed last night and there'd been no sign of used dishes and pans in the kitchen. He'd done all the clearing-up after them and she couldn't in complete honesty fault him for anything.

He hadn't tried to share her bed, to relive old times for just one more night, and she was trying her damnedest not to fault him for that! But the sorry truth was, she wanted him so badly she was like a cat on hot bricks around him, despising herself for it because it was counter-productive, not helping her on her long, lonely journey away from loving him.

When Cesare joined her on the bench her tummy flipped right over. Hoping he wouldn't notice, she carefully eased more space between them, and when he held out his plate of lavishly buttered toast to her she muttered, 'No, thanks,' and turned her head away.

The wretched butterflies would instantly reject anything she attempted to swallow, she just knew it, and because it absolutely had to be said, she asked, 'Why are you here? Tell me.'

'Why not?' Cesare casually countered through a mouthful. 'I found I had to come back to the island and you're stranded here for a few more days, so we might as well keep each other company.'

Just like that! And his 'few days' were too damned many! Didn't he know what his company was doing to her?

No, of course he didn't, she answered herself dourly. In the sort of circles he moved in the ending of an affair was no big deal. And, assuming the participants were civilised and sophisticated, they could remain friends.

As he was demonstrating!

Unconsciously grinding her teeth, Bianca decided she'd preferred it the other way. As he'd been when he'd apologised, agreed their affair was over and walked away from her, detached, cold, remote.

At least it had drawn a definite line under their relationship. This way, his way, was nothing more than torture!

Through a brain positively spinning with the helpless savagery of her thoughts, she heard Cesare confide, 'I thought we might take the launch out today, visit one or two of the other islands. I called in at the villa earlier and asked Maria to send someone down to the *Bella Alegra* with a picnic hamper.'

About to tell him no way, no, thanks, she took rapid mental stock, changed her mind and wisely kept her mouth shut. If she said she wouldn't go, then he probably wouldn't go, either. At least a day spent island hopping would give her something else to think about. She would just have to concentrate on what she was seeing and try to forget he was with her.

At least she wouldn't have to fight off—or eagerly submit to?—his sexual attentions! He was highly sexed, as she knew only too well, and he certainly wouldn't have kept to a separate bedroom last night if his intentions had lain in that direction!

'You'll need a hat, dark glasses and sun-screen,' he was listing as he glanced at the face of his watch. 'You won't want to get burned.'

She had already been badly burned. By him! Bianca thought scathingly as she went back to her room to collect the things she'd need. But there was still time to change her mind, she thought indecisively as she dithered about, pushing a tube of sun-screen, tissues and dark glasses into a padded cotton shoulder bag.

She could spend her regular twenty minutes or so

with Helene and the rest of the day at the villa with Jeanne. She couldn't see her restless, energetic ex-lover sticking to her like glue in that situation. A day of idleness, listening to her aunt's ramblings, wouldn't appeal to him in the slightest.

But the thought of deliberately opting for Jeanne's company instead of Cesare's left her feeling hollow, she conceded with a sense of defeat.

Like any addict, she thought despairingly, she couldn't get enough of him, even though she knew his company was very, very bad for her. Spending more time with him would be a serious set-back to a process of recovery that had barely even started.

She carefully kept her eyes on the island scenery as they walked over the hill and down to the cove to-gether; Cesare was naming the neighbouring islands he was aiming to head for and Bianca was too churned up inside to take any of it in. Only forced to emerge from her getting-her-nowhere thoughts when Ugo, car-rying a large cool-box, padded up behind them.

She made herself smile, and answer when the model-boy-perfect Italian claimed their attention with his *'Buongiorno, Signor, Signorina.'*

He slid to a halt in front of them, his eyes wandering down the length of Bianca's bare legs, a slow smile quirking his full lips until Cesare barked something in Italian that wiped the smile off his face and had him putting the cool-box on the stony ground, his head downbent, deferential, as he received what Bianca took to be a string of orders from his employer.

Watching the young Italian walk back along the track, Bianca felt her heart give a sudden lurch. Cesare's scathing reaction when he'd found her talking to Ugo yesterday evening had been exactly the same. Surely he wasn't actually jealous?

Either that or he had taken a sudden irrational dislike to his employee. The latter, she had to concede, seemed far more likely.

'Come, follow me,' he instructed with a terseness that was at odds with the lightness of his earlier mood. Then more smoothly, 'And watch where you put your feet.'

Bianca levelled him a look through the screen of her lashes. From where she was standing it seemed to her that the moderation of tone in that final instruction had caused Cesare quite a lot of effort, and his dark head was very erect as he carried the cool-box along the top of the natural rock terrace that sheltered the small, deep water cove from the storms that, so he now informed her, could come out of nowhere.

The launch was moored alongside, tied up to a sturdy iron ring concreted into a fissure in the rock. Clambering down necessitated taking his proffered hand, and produced sensations that she tried quite desperately to ignore.

The cool-box stowed away, Cesare untied and started the powerful engine and Bianca moved down to the stern, settling on a padded bench as the *Bella Alegra* headed for open waters, and blanked her mind to everything but the tug of the wind, the sun on her

face, and the green, green depths of the glassy, translucent water.

'This looks the perfect spot,' Cesare said. 'Don't you
think so, Bee?'

Whipping her straw hat off her head, she fanned her
flushed face, her smile spontaneous as she had to
agree, 'Perfect. And I'm starving!'

Leaving the *Bella Alegra* tied up in the tiny harbour
of Cesare's island's nearest neighbour, they had
walked through the tiny fishing port with its shady
piazza boasting a single café, past the humble pink
and white houses perched on terraces, and had headed
up the steep, unmade winding road until they had
found this small secluded cove with its crescent of
white sand and its backdrop of the towering rim of a
long-extinct volcano.

It was extravagantly beautiful and suddenly she was
fiercely glad she had swallowed her misgivings and
agreed to spend this day with him.

He had been the perfect companion throughout the
long morning, cruising slowly past ancient volcanic
rock formations, deep grottos where the water turned
a dark and mysterious olive-green and the silence was
intense, past weird and wonderful formations of hardened lava and gentle green slopes where sheep grazed.

He had explained things of interest, like the fact that
Homer had mentioned the islands in his 'Odyssey',
how volcanic eruptions over the long centuries had left
their coasts sharp and menacing within a mile of soft

rolling inland hills. She had found his knowledge of this constellation of little islands hugely fascinating.

Now he extended one lean, tanned hand. 'Hold onto me and we'll soon satisfy your appetite.' The huskily intimate tone of that sexily accented voice of his made her catch her breath with a fierce and forceful longing.

Taking his hand as they clambered down the narrow, steep track to the beach so far below, she told herself firmly not to read anything into that statement. How could she when he'd been the perfect gentleman, charming, entertaining, never touching her unnecessarily or giving her that smouldering look that had always emptied her mind of everything except the driving, insistent need to make love with him?

But the simple clasp of his hand, his long fingers curling around hers, made her heart expand within her chest and she could no more have deprived herself of his touch, his body warmth, as they walked over the sandy beach to the shade of a towering rock than she could have stopped breathing.

It was Cesare who withdrew his hand from hers as he bent to open the cool-box. Watching him, soaking up the sheer predatory grace of him, Bianca almost burst with emotion. Being with him was both necessity and torment. He didn't know it, but he was desperately loved.

As she sank down on the sand her eyes drank in his every movement, every glorious, gorgeous inch of him as if this were the last time she would ever see him.

His dark head bent, the tanned skin of his arms

glowing with health, and his smile as he finished what he was doing and handed her a loaded plate was her downfall.

'Thank you.' She could barely manage even that; her throat had closed up completely and tears stung the back of her eyes. She wanted to beg him to love her as passionately as she loved him. But it would be a waste of time because he couldn't. Why should he shackle himself for life?

He was rich, powerful and stunningly charismatic, unused to fidelity, oversexed, with a low boredom threshold. Why should he commit to one partner for life when he could play the field with impunity? And hadn't he told her as much himself?

She swallowed hard on something that threatened to turn into a sob, and her body went taut as he came to sit on the warm white sand beside her. She was an idiot, an utter fool. Weak enough to beg him to take her back, to give her as much of his life as he wanted to spare her. Cretin!

Sure that she was firmly on schedule to follow in Helene's footsteps, forever wanting the one man she couldn't have, she gazed unseeingly at the food on her plate. Her ravenous appetite had now completely disappeared.

Cesare was holding out a glass of cool white wine. After a tiny pause Bianca took it, her fingers shaking. If she drank lots and lots perhaps it would blunt the sharp edge of the pain, take the sting out of the fizzing tension that had to be coming from her, because he had nothing to get all wound up about, had he?

A solitary gull called overhead and the sea curled lazily onto the shore and above it all she could hear her own rapid heartbeats, the snag of her breath as she fought to control her powerful awareness of the silent man at her side.

Wishing he'd say something—because she simply couldn't—anything to break the spiral of tension, she tipped her head back, felt her sun-hat slither off, and drained the contents of her glass in two long swallows. Then she shuddered violently because normally she drank very little, and maybe, oh, heaven forbid, she was like Helene, the life sentence of unrequited love driving her to drink!

She gripped the stem of the glass so tightly her fingers hurt and then his fingers covered her own as he took the glass from her and set it down on the sand. When his eyes met hers she saw something that looked like anguish in the dark charcoal depths and couldn't understand why that might be.

His thick black lashes flickered then held steady. 'Bee, we have to talk. I can't keep this up any longer. I have something to say to you.'

His eyes burned into hers like a blowtorch and a ripple of apprehension coursed through her. Whatever he wanted to say would mean trouble. She could feel it in her bones!

CHAPTER TEN

HE HADN'T planned this, Cesare thought on a shaft of
self-contempt as Bianca's eyes flared with something
that looked like alarm, then flickered and dropped beneath the intensity of his.

Today and tomorrow had been earmarked for companionship only, with shared enjoyment for all they
did and saw, easy conversation, a return to the closeness they had always shared. Without making love, or
even coming near it. And not the merest hint of what
he really had in mind, persuading her to marry him
when he knew marriage was the last thing she wanted.

But it hadn't been easy and had proved impossible
when with every breath he took he burned to tell her
how he really felt, what he wanted from her. A character fault, he decided glumly. Want something, go
right out and make it happen had always been his phi-
losophy.

Praying he hadn't blown it by jumping in with two
left feet before he'd given himself enough time to
work on her, demonstrate how good they could be
together, that what they had shouldn't be lost, he made
a conscious effort to lighten up. One thing was sure,
he couldn't backtrack. He had to go on, but carefully.

He dug the fork into the plate of chicken in aspic

he'd given her and held the tempting morsel to her lips.

'Eat first, talk after,' he prompted gently. 'I don't want you passing out on me—you didn't eat breakfast remember?'

He saw her lowered eyelids flutter, a muscle in her throat jerk convulsively. He clenched his teeth together. For a few hours this morning she had been back to the way she had been during the first weeks of their relationship: warm, carefree, vital. Now the wariness that had positively screamed at him since he'd returned to the island was back in spades.

She flicked him an unreadable look through her thickly fringing dark lashes, then opened her lips to accept the tasty offering. A silent groan wrenched its jagged way through him. He would not give in to the brain-blanking desire to kiss her until neither of them knew where they were! He would not!

Light yet logical was the way to play this. Appeal to her bright intelligence, not to her senses.

Carefully, he curved the fingers of her one hand around the fork and settled the plate in the other, picking up his own now unwanted food, giving it a glance that curled his stomach and putting it straight down again.

She was a highly intelligent woman and would see the sound sense of what he was about to suggest.

Wouldn't she?

He cleared his throat, the sound raw. He felt like a gauche, inexperienced teenager and found the unprecedented sensation deeply unsettling. Cesare Andriotti reduced to a mass of nerves, to speechlessness, when he was about to make a pitch for something he wanted! Totally unheard of!

'Bianca—' Thankfully his voice didn't come out falsetto as he'd genuinely feared it might! 'I want you to marry me.'

Her head came up. Her beautiful eyes widened. The light tan she'd acquired deepened them to amber jewels. She'd tied her hair back in a long, floaty lemon-yellow thing but strands were escaping, framing her lovely face with black silk. Her soft lips parted and he snapped back to his senses and lifted one hand to silence whatever it was she'd been about to say.

'Don't answer yet. But promise me you'll think about it?' It was the best he could hope for; it would take a lot to erase the impression she'd taken away from that initial proposal, an impression he'd subsequently said nothing to negate.

'I'm learning new things about myself every day,' he told her, his voice low and husky. He tried to smile but didn't quite make it. She had put her plate down and drawn her knees up to her chest, looping her arms around them—a defensive gesture if ever he'd seen one.

She wasn't looking at him, but staring far out to sea, as if she could ignore what he'd said by pretending he didn't exist.

He was obviously no great shakes in the proposal department, he thought wryly as he reached out to

touch her shoulder just lightly to claim her attention.
Feeling her bones tense, he knew a moment's sheer
panic. Battening it down, he found control and began
to share his thoughts with her. 'I'm not very good at
this, am I? I've never done it before, never thought
I'd want to. When I proposed that first time I shocked
myself. I didn't know where it had come from and
you were right to ignore me. But don't ignore me now.
Look at me, Bee.'

For a moment he thought she was going to ignore
that request, shut him out completely. He held his
breath, then vented a sigh of relief as she shrugged his
hand from her shoulder and turned her head, her long
golden eyes narrowed like a cat squaring up for a fight.
At least he had her attention.

Holding the glitter of her gaze, he went for broke.
'I know you don't think much of the institution of
marriage, and neither did I until I got back to London
after leaving you on the island. It hit me then—why
I'd asked you to marry me that first time. It was out
of blind gut instinct. I want you with me permanently
and marriage is the best way to make that happen.'

She'd pulled her lips tightly back against her teeth,
he saw, as if to stem a flow of scathing words. For
some reason she'd wanted to walk away from their
relationship—following the pattern Helene had set
over the years, distrusting men because it had been
bred in her? Not wanting to let herself care too much,
protecting herself? He honestly didn't know.

'Leaving aside fantastic sex, we're good together,

we always have been.' He had to impress that on her, that he wanted to share more with her than physical pleasure. 'The mistake many couples make is marrying because they enjoy making love together. Passion blinds them. When the heat of excitement dies down everything starts to go pear-shaped because there's nothing else, and they discover they irritate each other and end up disliking each other—and cluttering up the divorce courts.'

Was he making any impression on her? Frustratedly, he didn't think so. She was saying nothing, her expression guarded.

His voice raw, he stated strongly, 'We have more than mere physical attraction going for us and I think it's worth hanging onto. I know we could make it work.'

Bianca looked away, quickly, before he saw the give-away shimmer of tears in her eyes. His proposal was tempting, far, far more than he knew. But in all of this he'd said no word of loving her.

But why should he when love didn't come into it? He couldn't bring himself to say that magic little word, tell a lie. Whatever else he was, Cesare wasn't a liar.

Huffing out the breath she hadn't realised she'd been holding, she turned her head and met his eyes. Her breath caught in her throat, every nerve ending in her body tingling. He looked so sincere, as if he really, truly, wanted her for his wife. The very thought of agreeing to what he wanted made her head spin.

Knowing she had to stay calm, not let herself give

in to the desperately real temptation to tell him what
he wanted to hear, setting them on a headlong course
to the altar, she said as tonelessly as ravaging emotions
would allow. 'What you're suggesting—marriage because we rub along well together—is hardly rational.'

'Are human relationships ever entirely rational?' he
countered. 'All I'm saying is that ours has always been
fantastic. In my opinion, as I said before, it's worth
hanging onto. That's one of the things I learned. Listen
to me, *cara*,' he commanded rawly as she turned her
attention back to the horizon.

'Since I'm marooned here with you I can hardly do
anything else,' she muttered, picking up handfuls of
the soft white sand and tossing them as far away as
she could possibly get them to go.

Watching her, sensing her emotional agitation as if
it were his own, he stamped firmly on the impulse to
take her in his arms and make love to her until she
gave him her promise. It could be done, he knew that.
But that way the battle would be too easily won, the
victory always uncertain.

'Another thing I learned was not to despise myself.
I did, you know,' he said with soft assurance when
she flicked him a sudden disbelieving glance. 'I positively loathed myself that night, our first on the island,
when you walked out into the night. I followed, of
course I did; you didn't know the layout, the dan-
gers—anything could have happened. I was out of my
mind with worry. I'd already made up my mind to tell
you I agreed to end our affair. It was what you wanted

and the most dishonourable thing I'd ever done was to try to force you to continue with it until I decided to end it.'

Her slight shoulders were drooping now, as if what he was saying was too much to bear, but he said because it was necessary, 'I found you and we ended up making love, because we couldn't help ourselves. I knew, after, that I had to get out. If I didn't I'd find myself, despicably, holding you to your side of that diabolical bargain.'

'I'd stopped fighting you by then,' Bianca admitted heavily, remembering her decision to stay with him for as long as he wanted her because each day she was finding herself more deeply in love with him. She hadn't wanted to love him but had got to the point when fighting it had become impossible.

'I know, *cara*, I know,' he said softly, something catching in the region of his heart and squeezing tightly. 'The way we made love that night told me that. But I couldn't let myself take advantage of you. So I went. I'd hardly set foot back in England before I realised I'd left something important behind. You. I'm not a cruel man, *cara*. That hellish bargain I forced you to accept was down to the same gut instinct that had produced that first proposal. I'd do anything, stoop to anything to keep you permanently with me.' A smile warmed his voice and made the back of her neck tingle. 'So I forgave myself for my bad behaviour because at last I understood it, and came back for you.'

'How permanent is permanent?' she returned im-

mediately, her fingers curling into the palms of her
hands until she thought they might draw blood.
Helene's words of warning were ringing in her ears,
loud and clear. She didn't want to listen but she
couldn't block them out.

And Cesare said heavily, determined not to lose on
this issue, 'I'm not your father, Bee. You've had the
unfortunate experience of growing up around a mother
you obviously love, seeing her go downhill, go to
pieces, because of what happened between her and
your father. Bee—' he reached for her hand and took
it, holding his breath, his heart punching his breast-
bone until her fingers at last curved acceptingly around
his own '—life doesn't come packaged with a cast-
iron guarantee. But some things are worth taking a
chance on. Unlike your father, I'm not an uncaring
bastard. You could try to trust me.'

Bianca's soft mouth trembled as she met the dark
intensity of his eyes. He was so beautiful. All of him.
His lithe, powerful physique, the proud tilt of his dark
head and the hard, clean line of his jaw. And the
strength of those long fingers entwined with her own
was sending the familiar shock waves of sensation
through her.

She loved him so much and wanted to trust him.
Trust him to be faithful and loyal, even if he didn't
actually love her. He had put them both through hoops
of fire before reaching the conclusion that he wanted
her as his wife, which was one huge admission for the

man who'd openly stated he saw no reason for surrendering his bachelor freedom.

Surely, in return, she could trust him?

She'd trusted him implicitly when he'd said that despite the ending of their relationship her mother would continue to get the specialist help she needed from Professor Vaccari.

Couldn't she just as easily trust him on this?

She really, really wanted to!

Tears welled and spilled over as she gave an emotional gulp, and, groaning, feeling as if his heart were being torn apart, Cesare folded her in his arms and held her, whispering driven endearments in his own language.

Her head cradled against the hard, muscular wall of his chest, Bianca listened to the sensual sounds of his native Italian, heard the heavy beat of his heart and just melted and looped her arms around his neck, her fingertips wandering feverishly in the short crisp hair at his nape.

Cesare gave a groan of satisfaction and gathered her more closely, his hands skimming from her shoulders down to her tiny waist, grazing the sides of her tingling breasts. 'Don't cry, *cara mia*,' he husked. 'I can't bear it.'

'I'm not crying,' Bianca lied, gulping back another rising sob. 'I'm—I'm just confused!'

Not knowing whether she was on her head or on her heels, fighting a battle with herself. But she knew she was losing when he brought his hands up to cup her cheekbones, mesmerising her with the steadfast power of his eyes, the firm, unsmiling line of his chis-elled mouth.

'Don't be,' he strictured. 'Just think about what I said. That's all I ask. You have four more days and nights to reach the conclusion I have. That we're hap-pier together than we are apart.'

She closed her eyes to block out the hypnotic temp-tation of him, of what he was asking of her. Her fin-gers stilled and splayed, pressing against his head. The touch of his hands set her on fire, promising heaven, but still no word of love.

If he said he was in love with her she'd take the chance. But he never would. And would the rest—sexual compatibility, close friendship, precious and important though that was—be enough to keep him with her throughout their lives?

If, in the future, he did fall in love for the first time, with someone else, or simply grew bored with a re-lationship that had grown tired once passion had faded, and left her, then her life wouldn't be worth a row of beans.

Just as her mother's hadn't been worth living after the only man she had ever loved had walked out on her.

Bianca shuddered, the lump in her throat threatening to choke her until she felt Cesare's lips, feathering over her closed eyelids, and heard the seductive whis-per of his voice as he murmured, 'So sad! I am offering you my name in marriage, not a choice of methods for your own execution!'

He would think she was a prize idiot, overreacting to a massive extent. He had no idea how deeply she loved him. Her soft lips wobbled and he took them with his own with an explosive hunger that burned out what little brain she had left and her body became instantly eager, answering his hunger with her own, and there was nothing more important than this, this fiery response to the way their mouths clung and mingled, to the frantic way he was undoing the buttons of her shirt, his heartbeats matching the wild drumming of her own as her breasts peaked into his hands and her own fingers slid beneath the hem of his T-shirt, touching his tight, burning skin.

This was heaven, this was right. Her sighs of pleasure whispering into his hungry mouth, her skin against his, burning, exciting, silk against hair-roughened satin, the way their clothing disappeared as if by magic, the way he found her softly curving woman's hips with the sliding, sensuous drift of his hands and positioned her beneath the narrow, hard span of his and sank himself into the slick heat of her...

CHAPTER ELEVEN

BIANCA came awake slowly and stretched lazily, a dreamy smile curving her passion-swollen lips.

The bedroom windows were open wide, catching the breeze, the light curtains swaying. She could hear the distant sound of the sea.

Turning her head, her dark hair spread against the crisp white pillow, she stretched out a hand to the empty space where he had been.

A low gurgle of laughter escaped her. Cesare had risen early, probably because he couldn't take any more middle-of-the-night punishment!

The two single beds, pushed together, had parted company twice during the night, depositing them both in the gap in the middle, all tangled up in each other, in sheets and pillows.

The shock of the rude awakening, of naked bodies trying to rid themselves of strangling sheets and smothering pillows, sort out which limbs belonged to whom and which did not, had almost instantly turned into something else entirely, the melting into each other, the slow stroking and kissing that had turned into driven passion on both occasions.

'I'm going to have to tie them together with anchor chains,' Cesare had vowed as he'd pushed the beds together for what had turned out to be the final time. 'Or we'll have to squash onto one of them, or sleep on the floor. Or we could, at a pinch, get Giovanni to trundle a double from the villa over on his mule cart. I'm getting much too old for such shocks to my system!'

But he'd been laughing, and so had she as she'd stood by, her arms full of bedlinen. And at that moment, right at that moment, she'd known she would agree to marry him. What they had was far too good to throw away. It might be a chance, a scary chance, but she'd take it because she now couldn't bear to think of the other option.

After they'd made love on the beach he hadn't mentioned the subject of marriage. He'd been giving her the time he'd promised. She'd grabbed the reprieve with both hands, feeling lighter in heart than she had in a long time.

It had been dark when they'd moored the *Bella Alegra*. Cesare had produced a torch from a tool box to light their way across the island. And in the little stone house, with the lamp lit because they both preferred the cosier, more intimate atmosphere, they had finished off the contents of the cool-box, the bottle of wine, and Cesare had said, sounding pretty serious, 'Giovanni can collect the empty box in the morning. I don't want Ugo anywhere near you. He's damned good at his job but when I saw him eyeing you up I wanted to beat him to a pulp.'

He was actually admitting to jealousy!

DIANA HAMILTON

Possessive, Bianca thought on a whirr of something that put her on a high, producing the insane idea that he really did love her. Only to be followed by the flattening knowledge that Cesare was one of the most up-front people she'd ever met. He didn't hide his feelings or pretend he didn't have them. He said what he felt, and devil take the consequences, and always meant what he said.

If he loved her he would have said so.

Now, luxuriating back against the pillows, her mind made up, she knew that love could grow. She would make him a good wife, the best, make sure he didn't stray.

But hadn't Helene done exactly that—even to the extent of deliberately getting pregnant with her as she'd desperately tried to hold onto her husband?

Before that niggle could gain a firm foothold Cesare entered the room and she turned her head on the pillow and gave him a beaming smile, drenching herself in the gorgeous perfection of him. Intensely male, very, very sexy, his lean body dressed this morning in cut-off denims and nothing else, he answered her smile with one of his own that sent her heart off into orbit.

'Coffee,' he said, putting the mug down on the night table within her reach. He sat on the edge of the bed. 'I have used my brains, *cara*. I am a genius! All I have to do is remove the castors from the beds and they won't roll apart whenever they feel like it! But first—' he took her hands '—I shall make breakfast. Will you be able to eat some?'

'But of course.' She smiled at his suddenly serious expression. 'I enjoy being waited on. Besides, I'm ravenous.'

'Yesterday morning you were so pale. You couldn't eat so much as a corner of toast,' he reminded her, searching her features with his dark head tipped slightly to one side.

'So?' That had been yesterday, her emotions had been in a mangled mess. This was today and entirely different.

'So you might be pregnant,' he answered slowly. 'Have you thought of that? Out on the hillside I didn't use protection. I must take the blame for that. I was negligent, not prepared, and you swept me away. And if nothing happened then, then consider yesterday on the beach, and when the bed threw us on the floor.'

Bianca struggled up against the pillows, her amber eyes fixed to his. It was a possibility, of course it was. In the past Cesare had taken the necessary precautions, believing in safe sex. Something had happened, fierce emotions had seen common sense fly out of the window. 'Would you mind?' she asked.

'As long as you were happy with it, I would be ecstatic.' He lifted her hands to his lips and brushed light kisses over her fingers. 'That is another thing I have recently learned about myself. I want a family. Previously, I believed I didn't want to be tied down—well, you know that—Claudia, in producing twin boys, had done my duty for me. I was mistaken.'

'And now?'

The pressure of his fingers increased until it became almost painful. 'I want a family,' Cesare stressed firmly, even as his heart leapt with a sudden blistering surge of wild elation. 'If you are already carrying my child then you will marry me!'

That unmissable note of triumph had been a bad, bad mistake, Cesare chided himself harshly as Bianca pulled her hands away from his and reached for her coffee-mug, cradling it, her eyes holding his steadily. He saw a tiny muscle jerk at the corner of her mouth and cursed himself.

Shifting slightly on the bed, he quickly embarked on a damage-limitation exercise. 'You are sensible enough, *cara mia*, to understand that marriage would be best for you and our child—should there be one. That is what I meant. We would be a family, and that is important. But it wouldn't stop you continuing your career,' he quickly assured her. 'You are brilliant at what you do and I know how much it means to you. A full-time nanny would be employed, and I promise you I would not spend nearly as much time working. I would spend time with our child.'

Her expression hadn't softened. If anything, those golden eyes were now glittering dangerously. He swore savagely inside his head. He was saying all the wrong things!

All he was trying to do was to assure her that an unexpected pregnancy needn't mean she had to lose out on a single thing. That he didn't want her to be, or feel, trapped.

In sheer desperation he tried to inject a note of levity, something to bring her back to him again. 'I think I would make a wonderful house-husband!'

It didn't raise the smallest smile, a joking agreement that he would look great in a pinny, a frying-pan in one hand and a squalling baby in the other.

'It's far too early to talk about pregnancy, or lay down orders about what I would be expected to do.' Bianca forced the words out through lips that felt as stiff as lumps of wood. 'And if you don't mind, please leave. I'd like to shower and dress.'

Cesare's head came up and his shoulders went rigid. Without another word he stood up and walked out of the room and Bianca glared at his retreating back, at the proud angle of his head, with mutiny in her eyes.

So he didn't like being dismissed. Well, tough! And he arrogantly thought he could call all the shots. Well, he couldn't!

Putting her cooling coffee back on the night table, she shot out of bed.

Had it suddenly struck him, back in London, that she might have conceived? Was that why he'd come back to the island and proposed?

Not because, as he'd so convincingly said, what they had together was too good to lose—but because, although he didn't mind losing her and what he had fatuously reported as being so wonderful about their relationship—as he had clearly demonstrated when he'd walked out on her and told her he agreed to the ending of their affair—if there was to be a child from that night on the hillside, he didn't want to lose it!

All Italian men wanted children, didn't they? They doted on them. It had just taken Cesare longer than most to recognise it. Faced with the possibility of a child, he had been taken over by his Italian genes. She was just a necessary appendage!

He didn't love her, but he would love their child with a mind-blowing extravagance and would probably burst with pride the first time he held it in his arms!

Although their child was probably nothing more than a wish for him, one that he hadn't known he'd had, he had got everything planned. He would re-schedule his work, delegate a lot more, to spend time with it while she, an out-of-focus blob on the periphery of that close little circle, could take herself off to work, keep out of the way until night-time, when he would do his best to father another child with her because he would have become addicted to the idea of his own family and wanted a whole horde of children in his own conceited image!

Catching a glimpse of her red-with-temper face in the mirror, she made a determined effort to calm herself down. She was being hysterical, twisting things.

There was almost certainly a thread of truth in the fabric of her thoughts, but could she really believe, after the sincerity of what he'd said yesterday, that she was completely unimportant to him, except as the possible carrier of his child?

She would ask him, demand the truth, but only when she was sufficiently calm to speak and act rationally.

Marrying him because he truly valued their relationship, as he'd said, was one thing. She could go along with that and hope that he would learn to love her if only half as much as she loved him.

Marrying him because that was the only way he could get complete control over their baby—sole control if she did as he obviously expected her to do and continued with a demanding career that often kept her at work well into the night—would be simply untenable.

And even if she wasn't pregnant, would the pattern emerge when she did conceive and produce a child?

Switching the shower on at full blast, she drowned out her groan of self-disgust. She was doing it again, attributing devious motives when without asking point-blank she had no way of knowing the truth of what he was thinking.

'Would you like more coffee?' Cesare asked, his voice chillingly polite, cutting right through her, sending a shiver down her spine.

Bianca shook her head numbly. She had damaged his pride and hated being at odds with him. Their warmth, their closeness, had been the thing she'd valued most highly during their relationship.

He had produced scrambled eggs and orange juice for breakfast and they had eaten in a silence punctuated now and then with stilted remarks about the weather, the supplies they were running low on and must remember to ask Giovanni to carry over from the villa.

A day of skirting warily around each other was not to be thought of, and Bianca knew that if they didn't get talking soon she would explode.

So now was the time to find out what really lay behind his proposal of marriage. Strive for an easy tone, nothing in the least way confrontational. 'Cesare, may I ask you something?'

'Anything!' His heart jerked inside him. The frost he'd put in her eyes with his blundering had melted. Her lovely features so earnest instead of frozen with contempt. Now was the time to try to redeem himself, explain that he'd only been thinking of her, of what she wanted because she was the only important consideration in his life.

He smiled for her in relief and wondered if she could see the love in his eyes, and if she'd welcome it or shy away from it because she didn't want the depth and responsibility of an emotion she couldn't return. 'Ask away.'

The tip of her tongue peeped out to moisten her lips and the look she slanted at him through the heavy, dark veil of her lashes was open and direct. He reached for her hand across the table and just as their fingers touched an irritating burbling from his mobile phone brought his slashing brows together in a frown.

'You left it on the dresser,' Bianca told him when

his scowl deepened as he turned his head and sought the source of the untimely interruption.

She gently withdrew her fingers from his. 'You should have turned it off,' she told him, grinning at the way he struck the side of his head with the heel of his palm before pushing back his chair and stalking across the room.

Very few people had his private mobile number. His parents, his sister and his executive PA. It had better be more than a mere babble of chatter to excuse this attack on his privacy at such a moment.

It was. He listened in grim silence for a few moments, barked a few terse words, switched off and vented a stream of what Bianca could only assume to be colourful Italian curses.

'Trouble?' she asked when the tirade subsided. And that was probably a huge understatement because he pulled in a deep breath that expanded his muscular chest and sucked in his washboard-hard stomach.

'Trouble I could do without,' he conceded, his eyes softening as his gaze feathered her face. 'Especially now. *Cara*—' he walked back to her, took her hands and drew her to her feet '—my chief accountant has been caught with his fingers in the till. The police are involved. I have to fly to Rome. Today. Now.'

His hands lifting to either side of her head, his fingers tangling in her hair, he lifted her face and said rawly, 'I'll be gone for a few days, a week at most. Promise me you'll wait? Cancel that flight? Ugo will see Jeanne safely onto the plane. Wait here for me?'

Her throat convulsed. Cancel that flight back to a normal getting-on-with-her-life situation when nothing had been resolved about his true reasons for wanting her to marry him. Surely that would be equivalent to saying yes, buying a pig in a poke? And as if he'd read her mind, answered her question, he said heavily, 'If you're not here when I get back I'll know you've thought about my proposal and have decided to reject it.' His fingers curved around her cheekbones, his eyes stricken as he warned tautly, 'In that event, and if you prove to be pregnant, then I will want, and get, equal rights in the care of our child. But I beg you, wait for me,' he breathed roughly, then dropped an achingly slow kiss on her mouth before releasing her abruptly and going up to change, taking the stairs two at a time, leaving Bianca staring after him, her mind in a muddle, swimming with all those unasked questions.

CHAPTER TWELVE

THE sense of doom was overwhelming. Despite the brilliant sunshine, the sparkling tranquil sea and the lazy peacefulness of the island, the feeling of it persisted, pressing down on Bianca until she didn't know what to do with herself.

For two whole days now she'd asked herself the same questions over and over again and got precisely nowhere.

If only that wretchedly intruding phone call had come through fifteen minutes later she would now know exactly where she stood.

A convenient body for all those children Cesare, in his extravagant Latin way, had now decided he wanted? Convenient because they were mostly on the same wavelength and the sex was great. Someone who could be sidelined, safely out of the way while she continued her career, while he hired a nanny to look after her children and he wallowed in the living evidence of his own virility?

Or would she be valued for herself?

Sometimes she thought the former. At other times she was sure of the latter.

If she could have had the time to ask him, would he have told the truth?

Of course he would, Bianca assured herself firmly. He didn't tell lies. She slapped the bowl of salad she'd been haphazardly preparing down on the work surface. He'd been frighteningly up-front about what would happen if she proved to be pregnant and rejected him.

Equal rights. Or perhaps sole custody? The very thought chilled her.

Unconsciously, she put her hand on her flat tummy. They were both jumping the gun here; she was in the middle of her cycle, or thereabouts. They would both have to wait to be sure. If she missed her next period she would buy one of those testing kits...

Then the thought that she was probably not pregnant at all made her bones go weak and shaky and her throat close right up.

She actually did want Cesare's baby!

And did that mean she would accept him anyway? Keep her fingers crossed for their future happiness, tell him that if he brought a nanny in she would send her straight out again because, despite what he might want, she was going to be a full-time mum? That although he would have his say, of course he would, no way would she allow her baby to grow up to be a spoiled brat, indulged in every possible way by a doting father!

Convinced she was getting close to losing her mind, Bianca walked out into the sunlight. She'd missed visiting Helene since Cesare had reappeared and felt decidedly guilty, so she would walk across to the villa and invite herself for lunch, spend some time with her mother and tell Jeanne that she wouldn't be returning to the UK with her after all.

You owe it to Cesare—and let's face it, to yourself, too—to stay, to hear what he has to say, she told herself.

Lunch was already in progress, on the terrace as usual. Marco handed her into a vacant chair while Maria bustled forwards to lay an extra place.

'What a surprise!' Helene's greeting was acid. 'Where have you been? It's been two days since Signor Andriotti flew himself off again.'

Her mouth took on the petulant droop Bianca dreaded as Helene added, 'While I wouldn't presume to claim a minute of your time while you had more interesting company, I would have thought you could have spared me half an hour since you've been left high and dry again.'

'Sorry.'

Bianca gave Helene an apologetic smile and the professor put in gently, 'Our children grow up, Helene, they have their own lives to lead. But they don't grow away unless they're pushed in that direction.'

He handed Bianca a dish of pasta with creamy mushroom sauce and said, 'I lost my wife many years ago and sometimes I don't see either of my sons for months on end. They lead busy lives, but I know if I needed them they'd drop everything to be with me.'

Bianca added crisp green salad to her plate, watching Helene. She was looking at Marco Vaccari with limpid eyes but her mouth was still sulky. Her mother had relied on her for so many things over the years, for support—both emotional and practical—and, latterly when her money had run out, financially as well.

It had been a drain on her energy, her resources, Bianca admitted silently, and hoped the professor could work some kind of miracle and help Helene grow into a happy, self-reliant woman.

But if that didn't happen then she would have to be around, trying to stitch the pieces together. She loved her mother far too much to abandon her.

Her simmering rage against her father, the man whose behaviour had pushed his wife to the brink, was broken by Jeanne's practical, 'Have you done your packing yet, Bianca?'

'No.' Bianca swallowed a mouthful of the delicious pasta. The timing was a bit off, but she would have to tell them.

Glancing around the table, she said steadily, 'I won't be leaving with you after all. That's what I came to tell you. The plans have been changed. I'll be staying on here at least until Cesare gets back from Rome, and probably for a few days longer.'

She waited for Helene's explosion.

It came quickly. Her mother dropped her fork with a clatter, dark colour staining her face. 'You can't stay.' Her voice was thin and high.

'The arrangements have all been made, you can't just cancel them! You told me your affair was over, so why are you hanging around, waiting for him? I've nothing against him personally, how could I have when he's been so generous to all of us? But he'll hurt you in the end, if you let him. Look at what's happening now! He's obviously giving you the run-around! Besides...' she played her trump card '...as soon as your flight was booked, I phoned Stazia Lynley and told her you'd be back at work next week. She was very relieved; you can't let her down. Do you intend to lose your job because some man's dangling you on a piece of string?' Her voice was rising hysterically now, her hands shaking.

Bianca's heart plummeted. Whenever Helene looked at Cesare Andriotti she saw danger for her daughter, saw her own sorry history repeating itself. It was irrational, of course, but a part of her neurosis. And Bianca's having been constantly exposed from her earliest years, some of it had rubbed off on her.

Inwardly shaking, Bianca reached over the table and touched Helene's hand. 'Cesare wouldn't deliberately hurt me,' she attempted to soothe. 'Or anyone else, for that matter. He's not that type of man.'

And knew with a deeply felt conviction that it was the truth. His reasons for wanting to marry her weren't based on love, but they were genuine, and, even if they stemmed solely from the fact that she might be pregnant and he wanted his child, he would never try to hurt her. He wasn't a cruel man.

He had tried to be, but in the end his sense of what was right had stopped him.

'Believe me, I wouldn't stay on here if I thought he was giving me the run-around!' Her words had been meant to comfort her mother, lighten the tension. But Helene jerked to her feet, knocking her chair over as she fled back into the house.

'Don't—let her go. It is for the best.' Marco laid a restraining hand on Bianca's arm as she rose to follow. 'One of the things Helene has to learn is that you will not always be around to dry her tears and make everything safe for her again.'

Jeanne shrugged her plump shoulders and helped herself from the fruit bowl. 'And there was me, thinking she was improving! Eating better and putting on some weight and not climbing the walls because she can't have a drink!'

Marco smiled, leaning back in his chair. 'Your sister's not an alcoholic. She used drink as a crutch. When she no longer needs a crutch she will be able to have the occasional social drink without any ill effects whatsoever. And she's had a difficult morning.' His kind eyes turned to Bianca. 'It's been the first tough session of her counselling, so you mustn't mind her tantrum! She is making progress, and she will progress much further. But it will take time.'

Which was something of a comfort, Bianca consoled herself as the lunch party broke up and she accompanied Jeanne to the marble-paved poolside, settled her in a comfy lounger in the shade of a huge green umbrella, and left her to sleep off the effects of several helpings of pasta, a generous slice of banana tart topped with cream and a large number of grapes.

But how much time had Marco in mind? Would the

news that her precious daughter had agreed to marry Cesare Andriotti prove an insurmountable set-back? she worried as she walked back across the island in the early afternoon heat.

Because she would marry him, she knew that now. Whatever his reasons, hers were the right ones. She loved him and life without him would be so severely impoverished she couldn't now bear to think of it.

The clarity of her decision made her heart sing. Taking a book down to the shady, ferny place on the banks of the stream, she began the long wait for his return.

'You are here—thank goodness!' Jeanne trudged through the open door as Bianca was beating eggs for her lunchtime omelette. 'When you didn't drop by at coffee-time I knew I'd have to find you even if I did have to search the whole island! It's the heat—'

Jeanne flapped a plump hand in front of her red, perspiring face. 'And,' she added darkly, 'all this wretched weight I've put on! The food's too good to resist and there's nothing to do but sit around. It's just as well I'm leaving tomorrow or I'd be too fat to move, even if I wanted to!'

Smiling sympathetically, Bianca motioned her aunt into a chair and crossed to the fridge to pour her a glass of chilled orange juice, explaining, 'I didn't drop by this morning because I didn't know if I should. I would have phoned through to the professor to ask his advice, but I don't have the number.'

She had already used her mobile to contact Stazia and explain that Helene had been wrong, she wouldn't be turning up for work quite so soon.

The news hadn't gone down well; she hadn't expected it to have done. But waiting for Cesare took precedence over her career, over everything else, if she was honest. 'So maybe I'll come by later and hope to catch him alone. Or—' she turned, the glass of juice in her hand '—you could ask him for me when you get a moment alone with him. I'll give you my mobile number. I don't want to do the wrong thing and upset Helene any more than I did yesterday.'

'You couldn't.' Jeanne accepted the glass and took a thirsty gulp. 'Upset her any more than you already have, I mean. Personally, I don't know how much good this mumbo-jumbo counselling is doing her. She should have gone to a proper clinic, that's what I say. And pull herself together. I don't approve of you having a fling with that young man because I'm happy to admit I'm old-fashioned that way. But I wouldn't go berserk about it!'

'What happened?' Bianca felt for the back of a chair and sat down quickly before her suddenly weak legs gave way beneath her.

'That's what I had to come and tell you. Marco said he could handle the situation—I think he had to give her a sedative last night—he said that you had to make your own decisions. But it's my opinion you have the right to know.'

Bianca's stomach turned over. 'Know what?' she

prodded, prodded too sharply, she regretted as Jeanne's eyebrows rose haughtily.

'Your mother's insisting that if you don't leave with me in the morning, then she will. She means it and there's no one can stop her. Except you.'

CHAPTER THIRTEEN

His mouth tight with pain, Cesare endlessly paced the uneven top of the stone wall, staring out to sea, waiting for the *Bella Alegra*'s return. He had lost all track of time.

He had lost everything.

Bianca hadn't waited.

'If you're not here when I get back I'll know you've thought about my proposal and have decided to reject it.' His own words rang hollowly in his ears.

The woman he had learned to love with a depth and breadth that had shaken him out of his earlier, empty conviction that freedom was the one thing he valued above all else had walked out of his life, leaving him completely enslaved, wearing the shackles of unrequited love.

His mouth made a cynical curve as he remembered how he'd felt when he'd shut down the helicopter's engine, run through the check-list and scrambled out beneath the still-rotating blades.

Elated!

Returning earlier than he had dared to hope, he'd known she would be there, would have cancelled her flight out this morning. His beautiful Bianca would be waiting for him because what they had was so precious. He knew it, and so by now must she!

And if she was still undecided over whether or not to bind her life to his for as long as they lived, then— *Dio!*—he would do everything in his power to persuade her!

Reaching the top of the track, he had come face to face with his old friend. Marco would have heard the racket of his approach, he could hardly have missed it, and had obviously come out to greet him.

Impatience to be with Bianca, see her glorious smile, touch her, urged him to keep going, just a nod of greeting, a 'see you later,' but politeness stopped him, but only briefly, he told himself.

'How are things?' The question would be expected.

'Settled down now.'

The answer wasn't. Something had obviously happened while he'd been away. The chef throwing a wobbly? It wasn't unknown. Ugo causing a cat-fight between competing members of the younger female staff? Whatever, it could wait. His reunion with Bianca couldn't.

'Did Jeanne get away OK?' He remembered to enquire, as he would have done after any departing guest.

'Yes. Both of them. Her and Bianca.'

For a stunned moment he hadn't been able to believe it. And when the shock had worn off the pain had begun.

'Ugo took them both in the launch in plenty of time to catch the London flight…'

Then more, Cesare only caught fragments through the blind beating of a brain that was struggling to come to terms with the unthinkable.

She had gone. She hadn't waited. The message was clear and he wasn't able to bear it.

And still Marco was talking, bits and pieces that were of no interest to him…'tantrums and mood swings'…'giving way since childhood, I would imagine'…'regrettable'…'prognosis good, fortunately.'

He couldn't remember now, how he had finally excused himself, could only remember coming down here to wait for the *Bella Alegra*.

She might have given Ugo a message for him. Hope flared briefly and just as quickly died again. She wouldn't need to, would she? Her departure had been her message. No other was needed.

He swore savagely, bunching his fists into the pockets of his jeans, the sun beating down on his head, perspiration making his skin slick. And still he waited.

There would be no message, he knew that, but Ugo could pilot the bird back to Palermo, dump him there because he was in no fit state to take the controls. There was nothing here for him now. He never wanted to see this wretched place again.

He would head for his villa on the outskirts of Rome. Hole up, get drunk for a week to anaesthetise the pain that was cutting him in two. And then, somehow, get on with his life. Try to forget…

Sitting in the prow, Bianca willed the launch to go faster. At least the island was in sight now, a misty blob on the horizon. She couldn't wait to get back there, tear up that letter and wait for Cesare.

Ugo was still trying to make conversation, but beyond the nods and abstracted smiles she'd lobbed in his direction she had made little contribution.

He probably thought she was crazy.

Waiting to check their luggage in, Jeanne had said, 'Maybe you did the right thing, maybe you didn't. All I can say is, sticking to your original decision to leave with me settled her down again. She insisted on joining me for early breakfast this morning. She was bright as a button. Well, she would be, wouldn't she? She's got her own way. Got you out of the wicked clutches of the evil squire, or whatever the Italian equivalent is!'

Jeanne shuffled forward as the queue in front of her moved and Bianca went very still. Ugo pushed their trolley-load of luggage forward. Acting as escort to two women was boring him; Bianca could see that from his expression. One of the women was openly disapproving, the other unflatteringly impervious to his flirtatious overtures.

Ungluing her feet from the floor, Bianca touched her aunt's shoulder. 'I'm going back.'

Turning, she began to unload her luggage from the trolley, ignoring Ugo's almost comically raised eyebrows. And Jeanne said, 'What about Helene?'

'What about her? Don't get me wrong, I do care about her, but I care about Cesare more. He's asked me to marry him. He asked me to wait for him on the island. This is my life, Jeanne, I'm not going to mess up because Helene's riddled with neuroses. I've always been there for her, and I always will be. I'd do anything for her except turn my back on the man I love.'

Even if he didn't love her?

Bianca ignored that niggle. It didn't matter. He wanted her with him, and that would be enough because she wanted to be with him more than anything else in the universe.

'She'll throw a fit!' Jeanne warned.

'Probably.' The last of the luggage removed, her aunt moving to the head of the queue, Bianca added, 'Marco will handle her. That's what Cesare's paying him to do and I have complete confidence in the professor's ability!'

She had felt light-headed, as if a heavy burden had been lifted from her shoulders. Still did. And the island was beginning to take on form, a rounded green hump in the sparkling azure waters, it looked like a child's drawing.

Her tummy crawled with excitement. The first thing she would do when she got back to the little stone house was tear up that letter. She'd left it on the table where he would be sure to find it, sealed with his name on the envelope.

The words she had written, she saw now, were an open admission of defeat. Explaining the complete reversal of any progress Helene might have made when she'd learned that their affair was ongoing. The marriage proposal hadn't been mentioned and she'd be grateful if he wouldn't mention it, either. She'd gone on to say that she thought it best if they didn't see each other for some time.

She heaved a sigh of relief. Thank heaven she'd come to her senses in time! Then turned her thoughts to the happier subject of how she'd pass the coming days of waiting time.

After she'd disposed of that letter she'd change out of the simple oyster-coloured cotton suit she'd chosen to travel in. Put on shorts and a loose top, top up her tan and wish the time away, her ears constantly straining for the roar of the helicopter engine. And maybe—

All her thoughts flew out of her head as her eyes picked out the solitary figure on top of the stone wall that formed the mooring jetty.

Cesare! It could have been almost anyone, but she knew it was him. He was back already! As the *Bella Alegra* powered closer her breath thickened in her throat, her heart beating hard and fast. By now he would have read that letter. How would he be feeling? Gutted? Or just plain angry because she might, just might, be carrying his child?

And why was he waiting, his eyes glued to the fast-approaching launch?

Because he intended to order Ugo to take him straight back to Palermo, to catch the next flight to London, to track her down and not let her out of his sight until he knew whether or not she was pregnant?

That didn't make sense, she thought frantically. Not when the helicopter could get him there in no time at all, when his company's private jet was standing by.

Pushing useless guesses right out of her head as the *Bella Alegra* sidled alongside, she hiked up her narrow skirt and scrambled over the side and ran along the wall towards him.

His face was like stone.

It didn't matter—she could change it! She could make everything right again! And knew she was right when she flew over the uneven stones towards him, her arms held wide open, reaching for him, and saw the huge grin that transformed the rigid features to sheer radiance.

'Cara mia!' She was in his arms, and he was hers, she just knew it. His kisses were fevered and beneath her clinging hands she could feel every last one of the fine tremors that raged through his hard body. 'I was told you were on your way back to England. I was stunned when I saw you. I thought I had lost you!'

His eyes went black. 'You will marry me.' The raw words weren't framed as a question and, reaching up, she stroked her fingers across his slashing cheekbones, down to his hard jaw and over his passionate mouth, her answer an immediate and unequivocal yes.

His eyes flared with sudden triumph. He feathered light, teasing kisses over her mouth. 'I knew you would!'

'Such conceit!'

Her hand fisted as she put a mock punch on his jaw as punishment and he grinned and pulled her back into the circle of his arms, his mouth descending, making her whole world rock and she was clinging, her head spinning when he put her slightly away and said wryly, 'I was forgetting we had an audience. When

I'm with you, I forget what my own name is—everything!'

Which was a lovely thing to hear, but the kissing simply had to stop. Ugo was watching, grinning from ear to ear, and she just knew he'd be cheering and whistling, if he'd dared.

She also knew that the news of Cesare's marriage offer would spread round the villa like wildfire. Ugo had to have heard every word she'd said to Jeanne. Helene would go ballistic!

But that would be Marco's problem, she consoled herself as Cesare took her hand, instructed Ugo to have her luggage brought over, and led her onto the inland track.

Slipping an arm around her waist, he confessed, 'I was going out of my mind, thinking you'd gone having decided you couldn't be my wife. You were just accompanying your aunt, seeing her safely to her flight. Yes?'

Her feet faltered to a stop. If their relationship was to flourish she had to be completely honest. 'No, Cesare. I was leaving. When I told Helene I wasn't, said I was waiting for you to come back, she lost it. Whatever progress she'd made was wiped out when she vowed she'd leave the island if I didn't.'

Her slim shoulders lifted in a tiny shrug. 'What could I do? I couldn't let her lose this opportunity to get herself sorted out once and for all.'

'But you came back,' he said softly. That had to mean something. That she really cared for him, could even be falling in love with him? That she'd worked through the way she'd been conditioned since birth to distrust any man who didn't have a mortgage, drive a second-hand car, and live on credit?

Time would tell. He was far too cagey to push it. It was time to lighten up. She had agreed to marry him, hadn't she? That, for the moment, was joy enough. As they crested the hill he challenged, 'Race you down to the house—loser gets to seduce the winner!' and, without giving her time to draw breath, took the steep incline like a swallow in flight.

Pausing halfway down, he looked back. She was walking at a snail's pace, smiling serenely. She waved him away as he sprang back up towards her. 'Carry on—I'm looking forward to paying the loser's penalty!' she cried airily.

But he came on up, anyway, scooping her up into his arms, his voice husky with laughter and something a whole lot deeper as he told her, 'It will be a dead heat and then we can seduce each other!'

Which was fine by her, more than fine, she thought dizzily as he carried her over the threshold and slid her down the hard length of his body as he set her on her feet. He bent his dark head to kiss her with a soft and beautiful slowness and Bianca had scarcely got her breath back when he stated without the merest hint of compromise, 'As soon as the arrangements can be made, we will marry. And tomorrow I will see Helene and convince her that I am not like your father, that I will never do anything to hurt you.'

'Thank you,' she murmured, her eyes suddenly misty with tears, not registering what he was doing until his arm snaked out to take the envelope addressed to him from the table where she'd left it.

'For me? To tell me why you'd left?'

Bianca nodded, her blood running cold at the thought of what might have been.

'Is there anything in it apart from the reasons you've already given?' He tore the unopened envelope in two and then in two again, his eyes glinting wickedly. 'No matter. I have you; I have your promise. There is no need for anything else.'

As he strode over to deposit the shreds in the waste basket, Bianca questioned tentatively, 'I was about to ask you a question before that phone call, do you remember?' She would ask it again because she had to get things straight. But whatever his answer it wouldn't change a thing. She was bound to this man with an invisible, unbreakable cord.

'I remember.' He grinned at her over his shoulder. 'And I remember being enraged by the interruption! So ask away, *amore*.'

She ran her tongue over her dry lips as he walked back to her. 'Did you propose because you thought I might be pregnant?'

He stopped in his tracks, clearly taken aback. Then his sensual lips curved in a wide smile. He reached for her hands and carried them up to his mouth, dropping kisses on the backs of her fingers. 'If you think about it, I first asked you to marry me, back in London, when pregnancy wasn't a possibility. The second time was after I'd left you. I realised I loved you and had to have you with me for the rest of my life. I didn't even consider pregnancy until that morning when you looked so pale and couldn't manage to eat a thing. It hit me then that we might be making a baby between us. I admit to using that possibility as a lever.'

Bianca's mouth had fallen open, her face running with colour. 'Say that again,' she managed around the huge lump that had formed in her throat.

'I admit—and apologise for—'

'No, no, no!' She shook her head wildly. 'The other—you said you—you loved me?'

Cesare veiled his eyes and he looked almost humble. 'It just slipped out, *cara*. I simply hoped you would see the sense of marrying me and would allow me the pleasure of teaching you how to love me.' Then his proud head came up as he growled quietly, 'Of course I love you—what else do you think this is all about?'

'Oh, Cesare!' Flinging her arms around him, she burrowed her head into his chest, burbling incoherently, and with no small difficulty he held her slightly away from him, tilted her chin and brushed the teardrops from her flushed face.

'What are you trying to say, *amore*?'

'That you should have told me! What else?' Her hands curled round the solid muscles of his upper arms. She tried to shake him really hard but made no impression whatsoever. 'Why do you think I ended our affair? Because I'd fallen for you in a big way. I wanted out before I got in too deep. You didn't want love, commitment—'

He blocked out her words with his mouth and several long, soul-shattering minutes later he breathed huskily, 'It's all I want now. Loving each other, living for each other, for always.' He brushed her hair from the side of her face, finding the sensitive hollow behind her ear. 'I think it's time to pay the penalty we both owe for ending that race in a dead heat, don't you?'

Bianca could only nod, her eyes smouldering and her limbs quivering with the all-too-familiar sizzling heat as they moved, twined around each other, to the staircase. Only when he paused to take his mobile from the back pocket of his jeans did she manage to find a croaky voice. 'What are you doing?'

Punching in numbers, he gave her that heart-stopping, dazzling smile. 'Asking Maria to send someone over with champagne. We have much to celebrate.' The fingers of his free hand dipped beneath the neckline of her suit jacket, and began with supreme dexterity to undo the buttons. 'Shall we begin?'

Speechless, her breath taken away, Bianca could only nod, her glowing eyes telling him that things just kept getting better.

EPILOGUE

Eleven months later…

Bowls of golden daffodils decorated the large airy room and from the tall windows the view of the rolling, richly timbered countryside stretched for ever.

Bianca would never regret their decision to base their main home in the heart of the English countryside. It was perfect. She breathed a sigh of pure happiness as the tiny body wriggled in her arms. Flavia Alegra Andriotti was just over two months old and looked almost heartbreakingly adorable in her christening gown. She had a shock of dark hair and her father's dark charcoal eyes, incredibly long lashes and the tiniest toes imaginable.

Bianca's sense of soaring happiness was complete when Cesare, looking magnificent in his exquisitely crafted dark suit, came to stand behind her, clasping his arms around her waist, his hands resting on her flat tummy.

'Mrs Hammond has just seen the last of our guests out.'

He had insisted they have a housekeeper, and she'd turned out to be a treasure. As his wife, he'd informed her, she would have enough to do looking after their baby and attending to his needs, he'd added with that special gleam in his handsome eyes, needs which were many and varied.

His hands slipped beneath the hem of her sleek tawny-red suit jacket, massaging gently, and she caught her breath, turning her head, her mouth finding his.

He smiled that supremely confident smile of his, she could feel it, and the fingers of the hand that wasn't wrapped around her baby went to the ruby necklace he had given her on Flavia's birth. Diamonds were too cold for her, he'd told her. Fiery rubies were more suited to her passionate nature.

Feeling her body's immediate response to him, she could only agree.

Releasing her with marked reluctance, Cesare took their daughter from her arms and murmured, 'You may invite Helene and Marco to stay on for supper. But I warn you, love of my life, do not encourage them to linger! I have plans for an early night.'

Her eyes glowed for him. She was the love of his life, and he was hers. She placed her fingers against the carved beauty of his sensual mouth, then, breaking the intimate moment, she glanced over to the far end of the room where her mother and Marco Vaccari were relaxing in armchairs in front of the log fire.

Helene looked a different woman. She'd gained some much-needed weight, her hair was its natural honey-brown with only a hint of grey, and her make-up was discreet. But, far more importantly, she'd found serenity.

'Something tells me those two have news for us,' Cesare imparted quietly. 'Marco looks like a dog with two tails and Helene is sporting a huge diamond on her ring finger. I'm amazed you didn't notice it.'

Bianca tucked her hand beneath his arm. 'How could I, when I only have eyes for you?' she asked, dimpling, as they walked together towards the other couple who were too engrossed in each other to see them coming or hear Bianca's husky whisper, 'If they are newly engaged, I couldn't be happier. And maybe, they would like to spend time on their own,' she suggested huskily as his hand sneaked around her waist and drifted down her spine. 'There's that lovely restaurant between here and the next village—'

'That's my girl!' His hand curved around her hip and the usual elemental something sizzled between them. 'I'm sure they'll understand if we tell them our bedroom door is eagerly awaiting our arrival!'

He was incorrigible! Irresistible! He was her life. Smiling, she moved forward to muscle in on the last of their guests' murmured conversation.

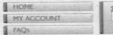

LOOK OUT...

...for this month's special product offer.
It can be found in the envelope containing
your invoice.

**Special offers are exclusively for
Reader Service™ members.**

You will benefit from:

- Free books & discounts
- Free gifts
- Free delivery to your door
- No purchase obligation – 14 day trial
- Free prize draws

THE LIST IS ENDLESS!!

*So what are you waiting for —
take a look **NOW!***

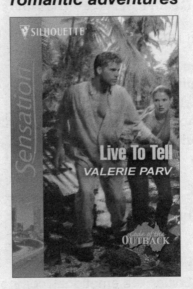

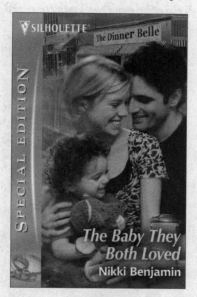

Escape into...

*Super*ROMANCE™

Enjoy the drama, explore the emotions, experience the relationship.

Longer than other Silhouette® books, Superromance offers you emotionally involving, exciting stories, with a touch of the unexpected.

Four new titles are available every month on subscription from the

READER SERVICE™